Ana Catarina was born in Portugal to a working-class family before immigrating as a young child to the United States. She has always looked to books for comfort, amusement, and escape. Creating characters and telling stories through them is one of her invigorating passions. She enjoys spending time with her family, most of all during the holidays, which is her favorite time of the year with its warm spirit of giving and wonder. She lives with her two children in her childhood home in New York.

Pen and paper kept me sane through emotional darkness as I sought out light. God's great gifts, my two beautiful children, were the push I needed to get through the darkness so that I could bask in my own afterglow. Along the journey I was draped in love and encouragement by a circle of family and dear friends who reminded me that I still had a lot of living left to do, and although a chapter was over, the book remained unfinished.

Bone deep gratitude to my 'circle.' Thank you for all the support and all the love.

Sempre p'ra frente, nunca p'ra trás.
Beijinhos.

Ana Catarina

AFTERGLOW

AUSTIN MACAULEY PUBLISHERS™

LONDON * CAMBRIDGE * NEW YORK * SHARJAH

Ordering Information
Quantity sales: Special discounts are available on quantity purchases by corporations, associations and others. For details, contact the publisher at the address below.

Publisher's Cataloguing-in-Publication data
Catarina, Ana
Afterglow

ISBN 9781647503857 (Paperback)
ISBN 9781647503864 (Hardback)
ISBN 9781647503871 (ePub e-book)

Library of Congress Control Number: 2024900718

www.austinmacauley.com/us

First Published 2024
Austin Macauley Publishers LLC
40 Wall Street, 33rd Floor, Suite 3302
New York, NY 10005
USA

mail-usa@austinmacauley.com
+1 (646) 5125767

Table of Contents

Chapter 1
Ava
Vilamor

There was no other place in the world that felt quite like Vilamor in the fall. Most people would suggest that spring is the season of rebirth and growth but it wasn't mine. The shift from summer into fall was always my season of change and this year, it meant more than any year prior because it marked three years since I had become a single mother.

I was ready to be done with the grieving, the pain and the loneliness. I found myself physically and figuratively in a new place that allowed me the freedom to shed my old self and discover who I wanted to be, because my old self no longer served me.

Autumn in Vilamor was something else, it didn't disappoint. The life I was building here allowed me to move on and it brought me hope. Perhaps it was the sunny disposition or the breath-taking scenery or perhaps just the old memories of my youth.

The day was clear with a bright sun that shone down, beating on the parched pavement. As far as the weather was concerned, it was a typical, uneventful hot day. The kind of hot that begged for a drink, any drink. Thankfully, the constant breeze brought with it a much-appreciated coolness that left me with bumps along my arms as it whipped down the olive-tree-covered hills.

What wasn't there to like about this time of the year? The grapes, among other fruits, were being harvested and all the autumn activities were a welcome distraction from the mundane life. The holidays, a new start of a school year, new fashions and weekends filled with bonfires and plenty of opportunities for new memories. This year, I was determined to start new traditions with my kids.

It had been just under one year since my return to Vilamor, the place I once called home and today was a good day. In fact, there have been more good days than bad days lately. That in and of itself was a blessing. Not too long ago, my days were gloomy and painfully hard to get through.

Why wouldn't they be? I grew up doing everything 'right'. I was financially stable, raised to have the best grades and be the hardest worker. Raised with a moral compass to do well and do right. To one day awaken, only to have the universe slap me with the reality that I now live in, was staggeringly difficult to accept.

I was, as they say, 'knocking on 40' and starting over. My finances were a disaster, the house I called home was in foreclosure and I was husbandless.

Life is good now. Not perfect but bearable. Decent. Some days, I would even go far enough to say that life was pleasant. Not joyful but also not gloomy. I lived in a small home that I rented from a sweet older couple and I liked it. I was fortunate with the kids' school and I loved my job.

My friendship with my cousin Gina was just like old times. Just as it was before we grew up and the reality of life dawned upon us. Those were the happy days before I left for my life as a married woman. A result of my marriage was that I had forgotten who I was and living miles away from home didn't help.

It felt good to be back on my old stomping ground. The kids had a great summer and I was looking forward to showing them a fun filled fall and holiday season in our new home. The best part of my new life was that I landed a dream job, thanks to Gina.

My boss, Liam Closter, turned out to not only be the best boss a single mom could ask for but a best friend of sorts. The sight of him made my heart patter, reminding me that there was still life in me and just maybe, there were better days ahead.

It was lunchtime on this Friday afternoon. Thank God! It had been a long week. Liam had been acting odd and his anxiety was giving me anxiety! I ran out to get errands done when Gina texted me that she got me my sandwich and was waiting at our usual spot.

I walked across the tree flanked courtyard at Closter Enterprises. I spotted Gina sitting at a picnic table under a swaying tree. I smiled and waved to her as I approached. She had already started eating her sandwich as she handed me mine.

"Thank you," I replied, taking the hearty sandwich from her.

"Why do I feel like you are always running?" She asked, rubbing her pregnant belly with a stretch.

"Umm, I guess because I am."

"Wonderful! Is that what I have to look forward to?"

"Probably not with one child but most definitely if you decide to have another."

"Ugh," she sighed, rolling her eyes. She didn't look herself today. Her usual peppy personality was subdued.

"What's bothering you, Gina? Heartburn again?" She hesitated, not making eye contact with me. She took bite after bite of her grilled veggie wrap. After what felt like minutes, I decided to press on.

"I doubt this mood you are in is all about my running around." I pulled back the brown parchment paper from my sandwich and took a bite of my panini as I mentally ran through today's events to figure out what was bringing on her attitude. I watched her, waiting for a response. A response that seemed to not want to come.

"Yeah, it's not," she finally answered. Gina was an auburn beauty. My mother was her father's sister but we looked nothing alike. She took after her mother and I took after mine. I admired her delicate features. She was glowing and growing now that she was in her second trimester of pregnancy.

She and her husband Luke never wanted kids, at least not until I moved back to town. They were the type to take spontaneous weekend trips and try every and all restaurants, bars and nightclubs on opening nights. Kids didn't fit their priorities but I guess being around my kids showed them what they were missing.

The next thing I knew, she was pregnant. She looked sad today as she spoke and I was growing concerned. She threw down her sandwich, suddenly disinterested in eating.

"Alright," she started, "you cannot repeat a word of what I am about to tell you." She pointed at me in a reprimanding manner with her red manicured finger. "You promise?" She asked. I nodded, making a cross over my heart with my finger and she continued, "Mr. Closter is retiring."

"Well, he's been discussing it, right?" I asked. Gina nodded with a sigh. "What are you worried about? I am sure it will take years for that transition."

Gina shook her head as she took a sip of her tea. "No Ava, it's like happening sooner than later. He has a stomach ulcer, which lead to tests and they found he has some issue with his heart. Both his doctor and Mrs. Closter have advised him that it is time to retire." She picked up her panini and took a bite. I watched and waited, wanting to know more. She swallowed hard. "It's happening like soon, like this month."

"Oh!" Now she had me concerned too. "And his replacement?" I asked, bringing my hazelnut flavored coffee to my lips.

"That's just it," she nodded her head, "I heard his oldest son, Nicholas will be replacing him."

"And is that bad?" I asked.

Gina shrugged her shoulders, offering little else. "What is he like?" I asked curiously.

Gina's eyes grew wide and she shook her head. "He is not like Mr. Closter or Liam for that matter." She took a bite, taking her time chewing and I hung on to her every word waiting for more. "He is good friends with Luke, they talk regularly. You know they are cousins but he hasn't been home in a long time."

"Wait. What?" I was confused. I didn't know Luke was related to a Closter. "They're cousins?"

"Oh, yeah, Nicholas Closter is Liam's half-brother. Nick's mom was my mother-in-law's sister. She passed years ago when Nick and Luke were kids."

I guess that explained why Liam rarely, actually never, spoke about his brother. So strange that he never once mentioned having a brother. Stranger still that there was a Closter that I hadn't met or heard of.

"How have I not met him?" I asked.

"You would have if you made it to my wedding." She laughed. She was laughing because I never made it out to Vilamor for her wedding festivities. That's the weekend nature took over and I welcomed my daughter a month earlier than her due date.

"I don't really know much as far as his management style. I see him briefly for holidays but other than that I can't really say. Luke says he is all about work, all day, every day. He lives, breathes, eats Closter Enterprises."

Gina wrapped the rest of her sandwich in the brown parchment paper. "Nicholas has been living in Paris for well over 10 years. Geez, maybe even closer to 15. He's in the Paris office, Client Relations and such. He is mostly involved in acquisitions. You know how that goes. He is traveling all the time, looking for opportunities to grow and expand. So, in short, I don't really have much experience with him."

"What does this mean for you? For me? Luke? Liam?" I asked the thoughts and questions rushing through me.

"I'm not sure, Ava." She looked at me with eyes of lament and sympathy. "I'd like to think we will stay on, hopefully in the same capacity or similar. I just don't know."

It had been eight months since first being hired at Closter Enterprises. Luck had been on my side when Liam, the owner's son, decided to hire me as his replacement assistant. Gina was Mr. Closter's executive assistant, he was the patriarch, president and CEO of Closter Enterprises.

It wasn't lost on me that Gina's recommendation made me favorable and fortunately after one interview, I got the job. I hit it off with Liam and was so happy to finally find a place that I liked working at. That then allowed me freedom to search for a house that I loved and could afford.

A place I could be comfortable in and proud to call home. Most importantly, Liam was accommodating. He was aware of some of my situation and gave me a flexible schedule. Now, I suddenly felt concerned that it was all too good to be true and I'd have to give it up. For the first time in a long time, I was worried.

Sensing my tension, Gina covered my hand with hers, "Don't worry Ava, I am sure Liam will take you wherever he goes in whatever capacity he will fill."

"And what if that's not here? Closter Enterprises has offices all over the globe. You said yourself that Nicholas Closter has been in Paris." I closed my eyes to stop the spinning in my head. Ripples of anxiety were riding through my body, bringing on feelings that threatened to paralyze me. "Gina, I don't have options, I don't have a plan B and if I lose this job, I will lose everything."

"I shouldn't have said anything." Gina bit her lip, concern seeping from her voice. "Don't let this worry you."

It was too late. I was officially worried. And now I needed to figure out what I could do to maintain this life for me and my kids.

Chapter 2
Ava

We returned to the fifth floor, the executive floor, after our lunch break. Upon our return, Mr. Closter called Gina into his office. She hurried her pace, holding a notebook and pen, turning once and giving me a wave as she walked into Mr. Closter's office.

Me? I was greeted with a yellow sticky note taped on my computer screen. It was from Liam. I recognized his handwriting. *Call me*, it said. Had he left? Had he stepped out of the office? Did I miss him? I knew for a fact that he didn't have any appointments today.

I placed my handbag and half eaten sandwich in the bottom drawer of my desk and rushed into his office. Thankfully, he was still there. He was packing files and items into his briefcase. He glanced up from what he was doing, facing my direction with a smile.

I loved that smile and loved it all the more when it was directed at me. He wore a classic navy suit, per usual, that contrasted perfectly with his golden hair but today, it looked slightly disheveled.

"Is everything ok? I saw your note." I took measured steps toward him.

"Ava! You're back, I thought I would miss you." He was rushing about in a hurry but didn't spare me his attention.

"Are you going somewhere?" I watched his swift movements.

"Yes. Paris," he said flatly. His fingers fumbled with his tie. He looked nervous, on edge. Liam never looked nervous. He was the poster child for laid back but this week, he was anxious. I walked over to help him as I often did.

"Vacation or work?" I asked, smiling as I looked up at his smoky gray eyes and my fingers went through the process of making a knot in his tie.

He put his hands on my upper arms and rubbed them softly, "Work, obviously and under short notice. I'm sorry."

"That's alright. You do what you must. Will you be gone long?"

"A week, maybe two," he said.

"Oh." I looked down to the floor and tried not to sound disappointed, hoping he wouldn't see the sadness in my eyes. After all, Liam and I were strictly friends but we had developed a deep camaraderie. We were close. Oddly, I had grown dependent on his friendship. I hope he didn't hear the displeasure in my voice.

"Don't be sad and don't be worried." He placed his warm finger under my chin, lifting my gaze up to his. "We need to talk when I get back. Maybe I can properly take you out?"

His hands returned to my upper arms. "Listen, you are going to hear some news around here soon enough. But don't worry, Ava. You will be fine. I'll make sure of it."

He stroked my arms once more. The look in his stormy gray eyes was one I had never seen. If I didn't know better, I would say it was the look of desire and before I could process that look, he pulled me closer to him.

His warm breath smelled of liquor. Had he been drinking at work? I never knew him to drink, not at work, not ever. Then he did something he had never done before. His face leaned closer; he was mere inches away.

I could feel the heat radiating from his body and his breath warmed my forehead. He lifted my chin as my neck arched to meet his height and then he leaned in and kissed me.

Liam Closter was kissing me! His lips pressed on mine. I hadn't been kissed in years and for the life of me, I didn't know what to do. It started as a sweet kiss that grew with intensity and it lingered for much longer than it should. This was not the type of relationship we had. It was the first time he had ever kissed me.

Sure, we hugged. There was even the occasional peck on the cheek, more often even my forehead but never during work hours and never on the lips. It was new, different and I didn't know what it meant or what to make of it. Better yet, how would this affect our relationship?

He dropped my arms, distancing himself and he beamed with a pleased smile.

"Ok, I have to go, the car is waiting downstairs. I need to leave now if I'm going to make the flight. If anything should come up, just send me an email or text and I'll answer after I land. If it's an emergency, call the Paris office."

"Oh, ok." I tried to breathe, to regain my composure as the shock wave washed over me. I swallowed hard and tried to find my voice. "Well then, safe travels, Liam."

He moved toward the door, turning around once before exiting, "oh, Ava?" He said as if remembering something.

"Yes."

"Wait for me," he uttered, "don't be hasty." He gave me a wink, then he was gone.

What did that mean? What was the hurry to Paris? Why did he kiss me? And what does he mean by not being hasty and waiting for him? I remained in his office much longer than I should have as I reran the events in my head. Liam Closter wants to take me out? I needed to tell Gina.

I walked down the white marble hall, my heels annoyingly clicking against the stone. I rounded the corner to Gina's desk and plopped down on the white cushioned chair across from her. She dropped her pen and sat back in her chair, looking at me with a puzzled brow.

"What is going on?" She said. "Where was Liam off to in such a hurry?"

"The airport. He is going to Paris."

"Paris!" She exclaimed. "Why Paris? Why would he leave now? Bad timing, don't you think?"

"I don't know. I think maybe it has to do with the retirement and all." Gina looked at me. She really looked at me as her eyes narrowed.

"Why do you look like that? What's going on?" She asked. She knew me so well, too well. I didn't hesitate.

"He kissed me."

"Liam? He kissed you?" I nodded. She banged her palm down on her desk. "It's about time!"

"What!" I exclaimed.

"It's been a long-time coming, Ava! What kind of kiss? I mean, you guys are already pretty touchy."

"We are not! It's not like that, Gina!"

"What kind of kiss? I want details." Her eyes squinted and she rubbed her hands together with excitement.

"A kiss! Like he pulled me to him, my chest to his chest and his lips to my lips."

"I am so excited!" She shrieked.

"Oh, stop! We are just friends."

"Yep, friends who call each other in the middle of the night."

"No, I don't like it. I don't like this. It just complicates things."

"Ava! He's hot, you're hot, he's rich, you need money," she laughed.

"What I need is this job, Gina! This is the best job I have had in over two and a half years. And now here he is talking about taking me out."

"He said that?"

"Yes, he said he wants to talk to me and take me out."

Gina's hand went to her mouth. "Oh my God, does he think he is getting the promotion? Maybe he is. That must be why he is going to Paris. This is wild!"

"I can't complicate this and risk my job. You know this, Gina. CEO or not, I can't start something with him."

"Stop, Ava! You always do this. Don't get all negative."

"Easy for you to say. I'll try not to. I just don't want things to change. I finally feel settled." My eyes started to burn. I didn't want to cry. "I am finally in a good place, Gina! I just want a breather."

Gina pulled a tissue out of a gray box on the corner of her desk and handed it to me. "Dry those tears and don't worry yet. There is nothing to be nervous about. At least not yet."

"He said something just before he left," I said, drying my cheek. "He told me to not be hasty and to wait for him."

"That can mean a lot of things. It can mean wait for him romantically, not as in don't be hasty giving your notice. I know how your brain works Ava Agostini, do not go there! Do not get negative and gloomy!"

It was too late for that. My brain had gone to that place and I now found myself searching for a plan B.

Chapter 3
Nicholas
Paris

A light rain drizzled down onto the streets of Paris this gray morning, making it much cooler than usual for September. Another early morning at the office for me. I was down to my final weeks in Paris with little time to spare. My office was a disaster, the same as my life.

My personal items were packed in neatly marked boxes alongside shredding carts and garbage carts packed to the rim with unnecessary documents and items that would not be accompanying me to Vilamor. My father's retirement, although long overdue, had been thoughtlessly announced and I now found myself running out of time to relocate to Vilamor, where I was needed.

I looked over my neatly typed to-do list, racking my brain for any details I may have missed. I picked up my phone, dialing my assistant's extension.

"Bonjour, Monsieur." The sweet voice of my assistant greeted me. That voice had been greeting me for the past four years. I wished I could relocate her too but she was Parisian through and through and had no desire to leave France.

Furthermore, my father's assistant was highly qualified and tenured at the job. Not to mention she was the wife of my cousin that meant I couldn't really get rid of her, even if I wanted to.

"Bonjour, Collette. Can you please get me a copy of the rental agreement for my apartment and then get the real estate agent on the phone?"

A loud ruckus came through the receiver along with muffled voices. Before I could question Collette about the interruption, my office door swung open violently, hitting the wall as my brother Liam rushed into my office, unannounced and unexpected.

"You!" He shouted, storming in. His hair was disheveled and falling toward his forehead. His clothes didn't look much better, they were wrinkled with his tie hanging loosely. He also wore sunglasses even though it was raining and we were inside. "You son of a bitch."

"Hello to you too, little brother. Welcome! I would offer you a drink but from the smell of it, I think you've had plenty."

I stood up and made my way around my desk, leaning on the edge. "Did you just come from a distillery? You smell like a frat house. What can I do for you?"

"You son of a bitch! You went behind my back and convinced father to give you the promotion. It should have gone to ME! And now you want to relocate ME to the Parisian office?"

"News travels fast, huh?" I motioned to the chair across from me. "Have a seat and we can discuss how spoiled you are and how incorrect your statements are?"

"I don't want to sit and I don't want to spend any more time here than I need to."

"Ok, very well. I'll address your statements so that we can both move on with our day." I shifted my weight, crossing one ankle over the other, preparing myself for his assault.

"Dad gave the promotion to the rightful son as far as I am concerned." I pointed my finger at him. "Why would you think you deserve the promotion over me?" I crossed my arms over my chest. He took three strides closer to me, his hands were fists and I stood my stance.

"Because I stayed home and have worked out of corporate since college, while you have been globetrotting."

"Globetrotting?" I asked, fully aggravated but keeping my tone in check. "By globetrotting, you mean searching for acquisitions? Then, yes. I grew the business while you sat at home living off the fat and by the fat, I mean Dad's money."

"I have a life back in Vilamor," he pled. "I can't and won't come to Paris." He paced like a rabid animal.

"Yes, you have a life in Vilamor and I have a life in Paris. As they say here in France, 'c'est la vie'. Someone needs to come head up operations here. Dad wants it to remain within the family and I agree we need someone trusted." He continued pacing, running his hands through his hair. "It's a promotion for you too, Chief Operating Officer. Cushy job for my cushy brother."

"I'm not coming, Nick! You keep Paris and give me corporate."

"It's not up to me. Now it is in the hands of the board."

"You can nominate someone else or renounce the promotion. You said yourself, you have a life in Paris. So, stay here. Keep your life, keep your lifestyle. You like to get your hands dirty with the acquisitions. You are good at it."

"I plan on still being involved in acquisitions and while I do have a life here in Paris, my goal was always to get back to Vilamor. I worked for that. I want to go home."

Liam stopped and turned his rage in my direction. "Fuck you, Nick!"

"Fuck me! You are drunk. Is this your new hobby? How much have you had to drink?"

"What is that of your business?"

"It's not but don't come in here intoxicated and spewing ludicrous, miseducated statements. Watch yourself, little brother. Your mother spoiled you to shit. That's not my problem. You've grown up to be an entitled man child."

"Don't make this personal, Nick and don't bring my mother into it!"

"I'm not, you are. You are the one who barged into my office asking me to give you the promotion."

"I was hoping you would be reasonable."

"Reasonable? What makes you prepared to take over? You do realize in most positions, you can't have your assistant do all the work and pass it on as your own. That only worked with Dad manning the ship. You'd sink anywhere else. Do yourself a favor and stay in your lane."

"Don't push it, Nick or I'll make sure you screw up. I will bring you down!" He knocked over a stack of my neatly packed boxes and stormed out of my office just as fast as he had stormed in.

I was never close to my brother. We had an eight-year age difference. Different mothers. Altogether different work ethics, which led to our paths rarely, if ever, crossing. Of course, he thought Dad should have nominated him as his successor, which was the result of his upbringing and overall egotistical personality.

True, Liam did remain in Vilamor after college, why wouldn't he? Liam could be summarized by one word, lazy. He got himself the quickest business degree, returned to Vilamor and continued living with his parents in my dad's luxurious home, helping himself to all the free benefits of that lifestyle.

He didn't take any unnecessary projects. Didn't travel unless absolutely necessary and at board meetings, he contributed little to nothing. Somehow, he still expected the promotion.

Now it appears that I needed to add him to my ever-growing list of nemesis. Sure, I could be brash, assertive, domineering and ruthless but never unjust in my acquisitions. One could even say I was generous in my pay-outs. I had put in the time and energy, giving my whole adult life to the success and expansion of Closter Enterprises.

This is what I worked for. I did it for myself and did it in memory of my mother. I didn't get words of appreciation but I think my mother would be pleased. If what I was taught in my Greek Orthodox upbringing was accurate, then I knew she was watching me now as proud as could be.

Chapter 4
Nicholas
Vilamor

Before I knew it, my days in Paris were over. Monday morning had come quickly. I was back in the land where I was born and raised. Back where I had spent my youth running around town with my cousins playing soccer, searching for raves and having beach bonfires.

I had so many good memories growing up in Vilamor. I had forgotten how most of the good memories of my life revolved around this town. I was happy to be back but damn, I had never felt my age more. I should bounce back without issue considering all the working out and eating well but that morning, my body was reminding me that I was in my 40s.

Pulling all-nighters, traveling and heading straight to work wasn't as easy as it used to be. The prior week had been a disaster, especially after Liam showed up at my office, drunk and raging over my promotion. That spoiled brat coasted through life and assumed Daddy dearest would hand him the promotion.

He was burning through his inheritance quicker than one could imagine and surely, he was looking for a way to pad his pockets. He stormed out of my office and disappeared. Not even our father knew his whereabouts. He ran away like a tantrum throwing toddler. My stepmother was to blame for all of this. He grew up accepted for his behavior and feelings of entitlement.

Now here I was in Vilamor earlier than planned to manage the unmanned corporate office. I had a vicious headache and my stomach was begging for food. A filling meal and nap were exactly what I needed but my schedule didn't allow for either.

I had little to no options with the lack of time, so I made a quick stop at a childhood favorite, Café Avignon, in the center of the town square to grab a much-needed coffee.

After twenty minutes of standing in line and waiting, I finally got my coffee and a ham cheese panini. I placed the loose change in the tip jar and walked toward the door with my mouth salivating at the smell of fresh baked bread.

This town had been quaint when I was growing up but now it was becoming overcrowded with tourists and expatriates who saw room for growth and investment. This led to long waits and crowds, especially in the center of town.

My head was pounding and my eyelids were heavy from the need for sleep. The aroma of the coffee seduced a smile from my lips and I couldn't get the cup to my mouth fast enough to taste my drug of choice. Ah, just what I needed, strong, black coffee.

I pushed the glass door open to leave and as I turned the corner of the shop, I was jolted in my tracks as I collided against the soft body of a female. My hands instinctively grabbed her upper arms to hold her in place. I caught her before she went down and took me with her.

"Oh my God!" Shrieked the woman. My panini went flying as the contents of my large, steaming hot coffee slid between our two bodies.

"Fuck that's hot!" I screamed on impulse. "Shit!"

"I'm so sorry!"

My hands remained on her upper body, holding her in place. It all happened so quickly that it took my brain a bit to catch up with my body. My brain finally jumpstarted into action. I looked down to assess what the hell happened. My eyes were met by the waves of soft, brunette hair that covered the woman's face while she leaned against me. It would have been a nasty fall if I hadn't been here to catch her.

"I am so sorry, sir!" Her soft voice exclaimed as she tilted her head toward me to meet my gaze.

I inhaled, seeking much needed air, feeling as if I had been punched in the gut. I was drowning in a tsunami of recognition. Even sleep deprived, hungry and grumpy, there was no mistaking the brown, almond shaped eyes that stared back at me.

Those lovely, warm eyes. Those were eyes I could get lost in. They were eyes I thought for sure I had gotten lost in many, many years ago. I knew these eyes. They were the familiar eyes of someone I hadn't seen since my youth.

I blinked rapidly, trying to regain my composure and find my words. "Are you alright?" I finally asked.

"Yes, thank you." Her eyes lit up as she scanned my face. "I should be asking you that question. I don't know what happened." She looked down at her shoeless foot and we both looked around to find her heel wedged in the sidewalk grate behind her.

"Looks like your shoe has been swallowed by the malicious grate."

She smiled with a little giggle at my stupid comment. Come on Closter, is that the best you got? I sounded like an inexperienced boy in this woman's presence.

I stared at that smile. That exquisite smile! That was when I knew. The memories flooded back like a 35 mm film. My chest tightened and I had to remind myself to breathe. It's her! It's my Frankie! It must be. I searched her face but she wasn't reacting to me.

"Here," I said, moving her weight to the stucco wall of the coffee shop. "Let me get that for you." I turned and after a few attempts, I was able to dislodge the black high heel from the slit of the sidewalk grate. "Here you are, your glass slipper." She giggled again as she placed the shoe on her foot.

"Thank you. I am so sorry. That would have been a nasty fall if you hadn't been here." Her eyes roamed over my chest. "I'm afraid your shirt didn't escape unharmed." She pointed to my chest. "Please let me buy you another coffee."

"No, I really need to get going, besides, it looks like I owe you for dry-cleaning. My coffee did some damage to your blouse as well." I stared at her shirt perhaps for too long. She looked down, her cheeks reddening. She fidgeted with her shirt and crossed her arms. "Let's just call it even," I suggested.

Her fingers moved to tuck a piece of hair behind her ear and my chest tightened again with an unrecognizable pressure as her face brightened with a heart-warming smile. She didn't recognize me, at least she wasn't reacting as though she did.

"Well then, thank you again for catching me and have a good day." Before I could further the conversation, she had waved and ran back down the sidewalk in a hurry.

I watched before turning in the direction of my car with no coffee, no sandwich, a pounding headache, an inexplicable chest pain but with a smile on my face like I hadn't had in years. I couldn't remember the last time I had smiled in this manner. It had been some time.

I got into my car, wincing as the leather burned through the material of my suit, making it uncomfortable to sit. I replayed the events and shook my head at what a fool I was.

It hadn't been the first time over the years that I had caught sight of a woman that I thought was Frankie and every time I had been wrong. But this woman today, I could swear it was her, even my body reacted to her.

Chapter 5
Nicholas

The drive back to the office was a blur. God knows if I ran a red light or even minimally yielded at a stop sign. Daydreaming would be an understatement. More like I was reliving a whole summer in that ten minute drive.

I had to get my head back in the game. I had too much to do to be mentally checked out. I flung open my office door to find my cousin Luke sitting in the chair opposite mine with a stack of files on his lap, ready for me to review. He watched me with a foolish smirk on his face as I walked through the door and marched to my chair. He eyed my coffee-stained shirt and didn't even try to hide his laugh.

"What happened to you? Did you have an argument with your coffee?" He joked.

"Ha-ha-ha," I said flatly.

"What the hell happened?"

I untucked my shirt and started unbuttoning it. "I ran into a woman."

Luke's eyebrows gathered in a crease. "Oh, is that so? Is that what they call it now? Was it an old fling? Or a quickie with a new acquaintance?"

"No man, not like that." I shook my head at his ridiculous remark. "I literally ran into a woman. Or should I say she ran into me. We collided. She fell on me. Whatever!" I ran my hands through my hair in frustration. I was shocked and rendered speechless by the recent events. I couldn't even get my words out properly.

"Her shoe got caught in the sidewalk grate outside of Cafe Avignon. Really, it is an oddly placed grate, it shouldn't be there." I digressed. "Anyway, her heel got caught. I saved her from face planting into the concrete. Can't say her shirt or mine were spared though."

Luke started laughing again. "Your life is always fascinating, cousin. You aren't even here a full 24 hours and already making drama."

"I am glad my life brings you so much amusement." I took my seat, turning my attention to my computer, I was staring at the blackened screen as I assessed my words. "The girl, she was familiar." I rubbed my chin, questioning if I should say anymore.

Should I tell him what I was thinking? Or would I just sound ridiculous? "Her eyes. They were a dead giveaway." I felt my mind wander into a daydream. "I've been with those eyes before, I can swear it but she didn't seem to recognize me."

Vilamor July 2000.

The overwhelming summer heat had brought on a quick, unusual rainstorm that afternoon. Rain was rare for that time of year.

"Come on!" I called to her from over my shoulder as I ran through the downpour toward the café. Frankie had been right behind me but as I turned my head, squinting through the curtain of rain, I saw that she was halfway across the parking lot. She was limping with one foot bare. She held her shoe in my direction, showing me the broken, black flip flop with a dangling strap.

"My shoe broke!" She screamed over the rain.

I ran back to her, picking her up. She was drenched. Pieces of her hair laid like papier-mâché across her rosy cheeks. Her face lit up with a giggle.

"What are you doing?" She asked as we bounced through the pelting rain drops.

"I can't have you stubbing your toe or getting a blister," I said as I ran back toward the café carrying her.

I'd never picked up a girl physically. It felt good. I felt on top of the world as I ran through the rain, holding her, bringing her to safety. Not that she was in harm's way but I felt like a hero, nonetheless. A 19-year-old hero. I placed her down upright when we finally reached the awning of Café Avignon.

"Let's hang here till the rain stops. We can get something to eat," I suggested.

"I'm soaking wet," she said, looking down at herself.

I shrugged. "Yeah, you are. So am I."

She looked through the window at the display of delights. "Hmmm ok. Their pastries look awesome."

"They are really good! All of them," I confirmed. "Come on, what do you want?"

"This is a French café, right?" She asked. I nodded. "I love croissants. You think they are good here?"

"The best!" I answered.

Luke shuffled, clearing his throat and it jolted me out of a decades old memory.

"What's this mystery woman's name?" He asked. "Maybe I know her from around town and can help you place her? After all, Vilamor isn't that large."

I blinked, shaking my head, "nah, I don't know her name. I didn't get a chance to ask."

"She seems to have left quite an impression on you."

"Yeah. The person she reminds me of left me with quite an impression for sure. Her name was Frankie. I could be wrong. It wouldn't be the first time." I waved it off. I played it like it was nothing as I finished unbuttoning my shirt, opening it to either side, relieved to get the sticky stained material off my skin. "Anyway, do you have an extra shirt?"

"I'll go check but if I don't, I am sure Liam does in his office. Ava's good about always leaving some of his dry cleaning here for these purposes."

"Who the hell is Ava? Is that brother dearest newest love interest?"

Luke started laughing. "No, Ava is his assistant."

"His assistant? What happened to Helen?"

Luke gave me a puzzled look. "Helen? Helen is 68 and retired a year ago."

"Why haven't I interviewed this Ava yet or seen her file? I thought we were done with the executive assistants. Get her in here and get me a shirt," I barked.

Chapter 6
Ava

It had been over a week since Liam left for Paris. I hadn't heard from him. There was no phone call, no text message, nothing. It made the waiting that much worse. The news had been made public that Mr. Closter was indeed retiring. As the announcement said, it was effective immediately, although no replacement had been announced.

The day was off to a crazy start. It was hectic as all Mondays were but potty training was destroying my mornings and I was a few minutes late. As if being late wasn't bad enough, I just had coffee spilled on my blouse. I rubbed at the coffee stain with a wet wipe as I walked toward the entrance of Closter Enterprises. Why had I chosen to wear white today? Isn't that the way it always goes? You wear white and get a stain.

I was aware I was power walking or 'running' as Gina called it. How right she had been. I was forever running. I made a conscious effort to slow my pace as I walked through the revolving glass doors and swiped my key card for access to the elevator.

"Good morning, George." I smiled toward the security desk.

"Good morning, Ava. Another spill?" He teased.

"You know it!" Ok, so maybe I am clumsy and more often than not have spills or stains but this was a SPILL, like the kind I couldn't hide.

The elevator doors closed and I rummaged through my bag for my scarf. I was tying the scarf as the elevator doors re-opened and I was smacked in the face by tension. There wasn't a soul to be seen and an odd silence took over the executive floor.

This floor, although busy, was always a fun, laid back environment. Everyone acted like family on this floor. But today, it was different. I walked straight to Gina's desk; she was pounding the keyboard as I approached.

"Good morning!" I said cheerily. She gave me a smile but didn't look up. "Gina, what's going on today?"

"Nicholas Closter is going on, our new CEO. Happy Monday!" She pouted.

"He's here!" I exclaimed, my hands moving to my disheveled hair. I certainly was not expecting to meet our new CEO today.

"Yep! He apparently flew in last night. He's been here well before 8:00 this morning I know because when I arrived, I already had this memo handwritten with a note asking me to proofread, type and submit for release."

"So, he's the chosen replacement?" I asked.

"Yes, just as I assumed. And he is hitting the ground running. He has already met with everyone on the executive floor, individually."

"Oh, shit!" I said.

"Oh, shit is right. He was just asking for you and he's furious you are late."

"Why didn't you text me? You should have told me."

"I didn't know until I walked in at eight this morning and let's be honest, you have the kids. You had to get them ready and drop them off. What were you going to do? How would it help you if I had texted you?"

"You're right. I'm sorry. I'm a little upset Liam didn't say anything." I shouldn't take my disappointment in Liam out on Gina.

"Have you even heard from him?" She asked flippantly. "He flies off to Paris unplanned and then is M.I.A."

"No. I haven't. He hasn't called. He has only emailed in response to things he's had to sign off on. So strange, Gina."

"I'll say. He plants a kiss on you and then you don't hear from him. Not even a text to say he landed. Maybe he's really busy with all the transitions."

"Well, what do I do?" I asked.

"Luke's in there now with Mr. CEO trying to smooth things for you. But you need to get your ass in there ASAP and get this introduction over with."

"Ok, so I should just go in?" I asked, pacing.

"Yes, because he's already furious that you're late."

"Well, I'm not very late. My hours start at 9:30."

"I know that. Most of us know that. He does not. Just go." She was waving me to get a move on.

"Ok," I said, turning on my heels.

"Ava," she called out. I turned around.

"Yes?"

"You have to do something about that coffee stain." She pointed to my chest.

"You can see it?"

"Yes, the scarf isn't working. It doesn't cover the stain. Come here." I walked over and she undid a button and tucked the two ends creating a V-neck. "There," she said, pleased with herself.

"Isn't this slightly inappropriate? Perhaps even provocative and suggestive?" I asked.

"Well here, we will put the scarf back and tie it," she said as she adjusted my scarf. "There! Better!" She seemed satisfied.

"Better, really?" I asked sarcastically.

"Listen, you're late, he's seething and you can't go in there with a coffee stain. You will look like a late, disheveled, disorganized mess. Nicholas Closter doesn't do disorganized or mess."

"Ok, ok! Wish me luck," I said.

"Good luck! Now go!" She waved me along.

I smirked and turned as I walked toward my new CEO's door. My heels tapped on the sleek, white marble floor that seemed to stretch for a mile before me. It was the same marble floor my heels tapped on daily but today, the sound was shallow and cold.

I shivered inexplicably with nerves. I hadn't even been this nervous when I interviewed with Liam. I didn't understand it but it felt as if I was walking into the lion's den. I had to remind myself to just breathe and get myself together.

I approached the oversized oak door and I was going to knock. I had all intentions of knocking but the door was ajar and I heard Luke's voice and a deeper voice, which I assumed was that of Nicholas Closter. They were talking and it was about me. So, what was I supposed to do other than stay and listen?

Chapter 7
Nicholas

It was now 9:45 in the morning. I was still hungry, seeing as I never got to eat the panini I bought. I met with every assistant and intern on the executive floor except for one. My brother's assistant. Of course, it would be my brother's assistant. Liam didn't have the best business sense and his desire to be everyone's friend had led him to the inappropriate choices for management and new hires.

I flipped open the file on my desk. *AVA AGOSTINI* was written across the tab. Luke brought me the personnel file in lieu of her, seeing as she was still late for work.

"So, bring me up to speed," I said as I flipped through the folder more than aware that my temper and patience were frayed from the lack of sleep. "Who is Ava Agostini?" I asked.

"She is your brother's assistant."

"Yes, we have established that much, Luke. Makes complete sense as he is the only person here who would allow this tardiness. It's almost 10:00, who is she that she thinks she can come into work an hour and a half late?" I barked.

"Right," Luke started. "So, Helen retired eight months ago and Ava was hired by your brother."

"My brother hired her personally?"

"Yes, actually she is Gina's cousin."

"So she has preferential treatment is what you are saying? She is young? Any experience? I'm not getting a good picture Luke, so please help me understand."

"She has a very good resume. She has worked corporate before, she is also a paralegal for over 10 years. She is good at her job Nick, give her a shot. She isn't young and inexperienced as you are suggesting."

"Hard to give her a shot when she is this late. What's her deal? Why is she late?"

"She's not that late," Luke said.

"I hate tardiness," I said flatly.

"She starts daily at 9:30. She has modified hours to accommodate dropping off her kids at school. She leaves at 3:30 to pick them up."

This was unreal, it just kept getting worse. "So, let me see if I understand this correctly, we have modified her hours of operation so she can drop off and pick up her kids?" I looked up from reading her resume to see Luke shaking his head. "She will need to arrange something with her husband. Six-hour days hardly constitutes full time at Closter Enterprises."

"She no longer has a husband," Luke said, fiddling with the files he held.

Now I understood. My little brother always was charitable and did have a soft spot for the needy and now here he was hiring an executive assistant that was a single mom and therefore could only work 6-hour days. Not acceptable.

"I feel really bad about her situation but she needs to go, Luke. Get a replacement ASAP. Perhaps we can find her another less important position, something not on the executive floor, something part time."

"I don't think we should do that, Nick."

"Why the hell not? Give me a reason. I can't have a part timer working for the VP of Marketing, it doesn't look good for the other departments. Who is covering for her when she isn't here? I'm sure one of the other assistants or better yet Gina, is filling in for her and that doesn't work. There is too much going on and the work is going to triple over the next few months with the acquisition of Laurent."

"She is good, Nick and I am not saying that because she is Gina's cousin." Luke paused to assess his words. "She is special to your brother. A friend if you will and he will be furious if you let her go."

Now it made sense. She was a 'special friend' of Liam's. Of course, charitable and a playboy, that was Liam.

"I understand," I said. "This is all making more sense to me now, so I have a gold-digging mom with two kids who happens to be my brother's 'friend with benefits' working on the executive floor of Closter Enterprises."

"No, I didn't say that. There are some rumors sure but don't put words in my mouth. From my understanding, they are just very good friends," clarified Luke.

"Very good friends? So, I can't get rid of her?"

"I don't think that is in your best interest seeing as you just got back in town. You said so yourself that he raged into your office. You don't want to ruffle any feathers, especially with your brother. He's already furious about the promotion. You have bigger fish to fry. We are hemorrhaging money. Don't you think that is more important than going after your brother's assistant?"

My head was throbbing. I rubbed my temples. This was going to be a long day. "Right, this is exactly why I am interviewing every single employee in this location, no preferential treatment Luke, everyone here needs to pull their weight."

"She is. Just trust me."

"You are vouching for her?" I asked. He nodded. "Very well, so I can't let her go? Then we will relocate her."

"Relocate her?" Luke questioned.

"Yes, maybe the wrong term, let's redistribute her."

I stood up to stretch my legs. I walked the short distance to the giant window and took in the view of the hills that spread before me. I observed the rolling mounds and how they were coated in vineyards as they hugged the cliffs.

The copper and golden limestone rock formations hung above the sea and greeted all who arrived at the shore with shiny, warm hues as they swept down to meet the turquoise sea. This! This is what I missed! I missed this view and what a great shot this would make! I stared out, wishing I had my camera.

This vista never got old and as I looked out to the valley below and the sea just beyond, I realized how much I had missed home. I had finally gotten the opportunity to come home and after decades of grinding it out for work, I now yearned for vacation. I yearned for space away from these decisions.

I needed to set a precedent and I wanted to take Closter Enterprises to the next level. That would take hard work and a dedicated staff. This, Ms. Agostini, needed to go and to be used as an example. I needed to clean house and it started with her.

But I didn't want to make the situation worse with my brother, things were already shaky between us. What was I to do? I thought over the dilemma and how best to handle it. I only came up with one solution.

"Yes Luke, let's redistribute Ms. Agostini. Effective immediately, she will be my assistant. Switch Gina."

"Gina?" He asked with concern in his voice, I'm sure he didn't want to hear that his wife would be 'demoted'.

"Yes, the baby's coming in a few months anyway, we will need maternity coverage. Let's just get Ava in her position ASAP."

"Very well, what am I to tell Liam and how do I explain the change to Ava?"

"Tell them that I need the legal experience that Ms. Agostini has and that the timing works perfectly with Gina's maternity leave."

"I don't know, Nick. If you think six-hour days don't cut it for Liam, why would you want to take that on yourself?"

"Because Luke, I can't have my lothario brother around a flirty single mom."

"Hey," interrupted Luke. "I never said anything about her being flirty."

"I can't get rid of her. That's what you said, so I'll just have to make it, so she wants to leave."

"You are going to push her out?" He nodded.

"Sure, if that's what you want to call it."

"She's a good employee Nick, she works after hours from home. Her work is done and well."

"Ok, let me see, let me be the judge." Luke nodded and walked toward the door. "Oh and Luke, it's effective immediately. I want it done before Liam returns."

Chapter 8
Ava

Sure, I was ashamed about my eavesdropping, no excuses it was wrong. I knew it was inappropriate but now I was just furious. This wasn't exactly the first impression I wanted of the new head of Closter Enterprises.

What a pompous ass! So, he was going to push me out? So, he thought! We will see about that. Mr. Nicholas Closter was under the impression I could be pushed out? Little did he know that I couldn't be pushed that easily.

I watched through the thin opening between the doors. Luke was coming toward me. This was my opportunity to let him know I wouldn't be bullied. Boss or not, I hadn't done anything wrong and he couldn't just push me out. If Nicholas Closter wanted to redistribute me, he'd have to tell me himself. Not Luke.

I composed myself, fixed my posture and knocked three times on the thick wood door. I opened it back and peeked in. I planted the most authentic smile I could muster upon my face as I let myself in. Luke immediately smiled back at me but I saw the concern in his eyes.

"Ava! Good morning," he said, rubbing his hands together awkwardly.

"Good morning!" I said, "Sorry I am late. Gina told me Mr. Closter has been looking for me."

"Yes, come in let me introduce you to Nicholas Closter."

I walked past the threshold into the office, closing the door behind me, as Luke moved to the side and that was when the Nicholas Closter, my new CEO, came into view. All 6 foot 2 inches of him. I felt a rush of heat as my eyes took him in. Before me stood the gorgeous man from the café. Our coffee-stained shirts matched.

Now that there was distance between us, I had time to take him in. He was exquisite. If that word could even be used to describe a man. He had black, perfectly gelled hair, with deep dark chocolate eyes to match and perfectly chiseled features that Michelangelo himself could not have better carved.

His chest and abs were out in display as he wore his shirt unbuttoned. I knew then, without hesitation, that this man was no stranger. The homey, familiar feelings filled me with warmth.

I don't know if it was in my mind but we just seemed to stare at each other. Neither one of us said anything. It was a stare down between the two of us until Luke shuffled and cleared his throat. Perhaps he did it to break the silence or perhaps it was a sign of the discomforting awkwardness.

"Uh, Ava Agostini, this is Mr. Nicholas Closter, our new president and CEO." Silence fell again until Luke spoke once more. "It looks like you both may have already met," he said as he pointed between our shirts. I looked down at my shirt and then at Nicholas Closter's chest.

"Yes. We met just before at the coffee shop," I said. "Although at the time I wasn't aware he was my new CEO. Congratulations, Mr. Closter and welcome. Your brother Liam hadn't mentioned the change but I am sure he will love having his brother in town more often."

"Speaking of Liam," Luke's voice cracked and he coughed to clear the frog in his throat. "Effective immediately, you will no longer be reporting to Liam but rather to Nicholas. Congratulations, Ava!"

"Oh, is that so?" I played along. "Liam isn't back in the office until the 22nd, shall I wait until his return so that I may tie up any loose ends?"

"No," said the deep, harsh voice that belonged to Nicholas Closter. I looked in the direction of the voice. The warm, welcoming, familial feelings were gone. Nicholas Closter walked from the window to his desk. "We are aware, Ms. Agostini, that my brother is out of town."

"You may call me Ava," I said, hoping to cut the coldness from his voice.

"Not necessary. Ms. Agostini will suffice." In that one statement, he swiftly established the type of relationship we would have. "The change is effective immediately. Luke will take care of the details and formal announcements."

He shuffled with papers on his desk and then brought his gaze to Luke. "Luke, you may go. Let Gina finish the press release and then she can start moving her stuff. Perhaps she can sit with Ms. Agostini this afternoon and review where she is at with her projects."

"Very well." Luke seemed to hesitate for a while. Then shook his head in my direction. "Ava, good luck." He winked at me and left, closing the door behind him, leaving me on my own.

My new CEO appeared frustrated, unimpressed and a complete tight ass. I started walking toward his desk.

"Gina said you wanted to speak with me. An interview, I assume." Nick cut me off. Waving his hand in front of his face as he loosened his tie with his other hand.

"Not necessary, Luke brought me up to speed on your experience and I will bring you up to speed on my expectations." He sat down, which did help to make me more comfortable as it decreased the height disparity and covered most or more of his killer abdomen.

"There are some changes I will require on your part. In the meantime, I have some errands that need immediate attention. Get me an appointment with a good therapeutic massage therapist. Drop off my dry cleaning; Gina has the address."

"Make sure the letters on Gina's desk are mailed out overnight with return receipt. And get me something to eat and a double espresso, no sugar," he looked in my direction briefly, "I didn't get to enjoy the one I previously bought." He rattled his orders in a quick, concise manner, jolting my brain with confusion.

I adjusted my scarf and it didn't go lost on me that he glanced at my chest, looking at the coffee stain or perhaps my breast. Either way, he was aware it was inappropriate and turned his gaze back to his computer screen, scrolling through his emails.

"Very well, will that be all, sir?" I asked.

"No, I need a new shirt. Luke said there may be some available in Liam's office. Get me one."

"Yes, sir. Excuse me." I turned to leave, not wanting to lose the mental list of errands. But something inside me told me I had to address his comments from earlier. I turned back.

"You know, a gold-digging single mom can be dangerous Mr. Closter, maybe even a gamble. But what a single mom has that most others don't is a need and a will to succeed because she is responsible for more than just herself. Judge me on my performance or lack thereof, not on my appearance."

I swiftly turned to leave, closing the door behind me before running to my desk to write down the list of errands I needed to complete. He wanted to push me? Game on! I'd push right back. At least until Liam came back. He'd fix this. I knew he would.

Where are you Liam? Come back. I need you.

Chapter 9
Nicholas

It had been a week since my return to my beautiful Vilamor. The routine was setting in and I already felt at home. At work, Ms. Agostini and I kept our relationship exceptionally professional with little to no unnecessary communication.

I didn't feel the need to get too comfortable with her as I knew she wouldn't be employed with Closter Enterprises for much longer. She couldn't for a myriad of reasons.

I was still in disbelief that the woman from the coffee shop was now my assistant. Better yet, the girl I obsessed over from my youth was now my assistant. My assistant who happened to be my brother's ex-assistant and potential love interest. Or at least I thought it was her.

This grown-up version was so unlike the girl I remember. Ms. Agostini was harder and colder. My Frankie was carefree and sweet. I found myself doubting, often even questioning if it was possible for the world to have two people that looked so alike.

Neither one of us mentioned the coffee shop or our youth but the more I worked with her, the more it tormented me. I struggled to concentrate. I had always been the one with my eye on the ball. Nothing deterred me from my goals. But this week, I flailed like a fish out of water. I was drowning with questions, curiosity and unexplained anger.

Consequently, things were not just strange at work. Things were strange at home too. My father had yet to make time for me since my return, no different than how it had been growing up. Sure, my father was lovable and warm to others. The center of attention for everyone except for me. Since my mother's death he had little to no time for me. It only got worse after he remarried. Then Liam came along.

My stepmother, Kate, disliked me, she always had. As an adult, I realized she disliked me because she saw my mother when she looked at me. I had the dark hair, dark features. I took after my mother's Greek side.

One wouldn't believe that Kate was my mother's best friend, odd, wasn't it? Kate was much too eager to rush to my father's side after my mother's passing. Not even a year in the ground and my father remarried. I was the constant reminder to both Kate and my father of their betrayal.

Liam came along a year later. He was the spitting image of my father. As a young boy, I couldn't understand why Kate didn't like me. I was 8 years old and just wanted a family and to be included.

By the age of 12, I was away at boarding school and would only come home for holidays and even those brief times at home, I ended up at Luke's house. My aunt Debra was so like the memory I had of my mother. She looked like her, smelled like her, laughed like her and those were real holidays.

She cooked all the old-world foods. Sure, they had less money, less material things than my own family but they were so much richer. Liam was my brother by blood but Luke was my real brother. We wanted what was best for one another.

We supported one another. We rallied for each other and there was no one else I would rather have by my side at Closter Enterprises than Luke. Luke was loyal.

I knew Liam was up to something. He made it no secret that he wanted the promotion. He wanted to be CEO and he thought he rightfully deserved it because he stayed home. Kate was in his ear and I am sure she had prepped him for that position all along.

Yes, I may be cold and a perpetual playboy and yes, I may have been in Paris and spent my time traveling but it was all for work. Every day of my life was breathing Closter Enterprises and that could not be said for Liam.

It irked me to not know what Liam was doing and not know his next step. He had gone to Paris and that was where he had remained going on two weeks or at least that is what we thought. I was fearing the worst, not quite sure what he was up to. His anger left me unsettled.

I believed Ms. Agostini was the only one communicating with Liam. She must know what my brother was up to. She had been his loyal assistant, from what I heard, both inside and outside the office. Now I was anxious to see where her loyalty lay.

I picked up the phone on Monday morning and dialed Luke's number.

"Hey, good morning!" He said cheerily.

"Good morning, everything ok? I noticed you and Gina aren't in yet."

"We're fine! We just have an ultrasound appointment. What's up?"

"I need you to do something for me."

"Right now? Your tone is already telling me I am not going to like this."

"I need you to look into Ms. Agostini. Find out if she is talking to Liam. When is the last time she has spoken to him? Find out what she knows."

"Nick, why don't you just ask her?"

"We don't really talk unless necessary," I explained.

"She's your assistant!"

"Right and I know little to nothing about her. Run a background check while you're at it. I noticed she never had one done when she was hired."

"Nick, I don't like this. She's Gina's cousin, this is family."

"We are family too, Luke and this is your job. These are simple questions you can ask her or have Gina find out." There was a quick knock on the door and Ava appeared.

"Ms. Agostini, good morning. Luke, I have to go but get on that and let me know what you come up with."

I hung up the phone and waved her in. She walked in, holding a coffee. Her ponytail, high on her head, swayed as she walked toward my desk. She was wearing one of those black skirts that hugged her curves and a red blouse, always the consummate professional. She looked good, except for the pout on her face. She didn't smile. We didn't do that, her and I, no smiles between us.

"Good morning, your double espresso, black, no sugar and your mail." She positioned the coffee in front of me and my mail in the tray to my left. "Do you need anything else this morning?"

"No," I replied blandly, turning my attention to my computer as she turned to leave. She was a few steps away from the door and I thought of Luke's words; 'just ask her', he had said.

"Ms. Agostini, have you heard from my brother?"

She stopped and pivoted, returning her attention to me. "No, not since the day he left."

That was surprising, and I didn't believe her. "You were his assistant and he never called you, not even once to touch base?"

She shook her head. "Never."

"Very well. Thank you."

She turned and I watched as her hips sashayed. Time had been kind to her. Twenty-two years later, she was harder, less easily impressed, not as open, curvier than I remembered but still beautiful. My chest pain returned, a burning, squeezing pain and I walked to the wet bar, to pour a glass of scotch, one of the perks of working for a liquor company. Sure, it was still morning but I had run out of pain killers, scotch would have to do.

I took the tumbler of liquor back to my desk. I sat down, holding the heavy crystal glass with all intentions of drinking it until I caught sight of the coffee she had left. I stared at that cup of coffee. I suppose I should drink it since she went through the trouble of getting it.

I reluctantly put down the scotch and picked up the coffee instead. I brought it to my lips and took a sip. I immediately set it back down as I shook my head. I picked up my cell phone and opened the messaging app. Yes, I had her cell phone number because I insisted on torturing her at all hours of the day, a tactic I hoped would push her out quicker.

Me: *Ms. Agostini, I like my coffee black.*

I watched as the message was sent and delivered. Three dots bounced along the bottom; she was typing. I waited anxiously.

Ms. Agostini: *Sir, the coffee is black.*

Me: *No, there is a hint of sweetness.*

Ms. Agostini: *Yes, it has a half teaspoon of stevia.*

Me: *Stevia?*

Ms. Agostini: *Yes, it is a sugar substitute. Much better for your health.*

Me: *How does that constitute black?*

Ms. Agostini: *It looked pretty black to me. No milk or creamer added.*

Me: *I want a black coffee, Ms. Agostini. Strong, black coffee, no flavor, no sugar, no additives. NOTHING.*

The message said it was delivered and read but no dots appeared after that message and no response came. Was she just going to ignore me? I turned my chair as I looked out the window at the view, thinking about what to do next or what to say when a knock came at my door. I turned to see Ms. Agostini walk into my office holding another coffee cup.

"Mr. Closter, your black coffee. Strong, black coffee, no flavor, no sugar, no additives."

She placed the new cup on my desk to the right of my paperwork, turned and walked out. I waited until I was sure she was gone before picking up the coffee cup. I took a mouthful and nodded as the flavor of the strong dark roast warmed me. I was pleased. It was perfect.

Chapter 10
Nicholas

I had forgotten to eat again today. I looked at my watch as my stomach growled with hunger. It was after 6:30, the office was cleared out at this point. After being almost a month in the office, it became obvious that my father should have handed me the position years ago.

Everything needed to be looked over, evaluated, deconstructed and reconstructed. But alas, it was getting late and it wouldn't all get done overnight.

Just when I was hoping to relax a bit, it turned out the Laurent patriarch was having cold feet about the sell. He had sent additional last-minute terms. I still needed to review them with the legal and financial departments but needed them added to the proposal draft. Nothing like waiting until the eleventh hour.

I grabbed my cell phone.

Me: *Ms. Agostini, Mr. Laurent's team has sent additional terms. They just came through. Please check your email as I need those added to the proposal.*

I put my phone down and rubbed my eyes as my phone pinged with a notification. I looked at the screen to see Ms. Agostini's name. She's quick, that much I could appreciate.

Ms. Agostini: *Is the proposal still due tomorrow?*

Me: *Yes, same as discussed, 9:00.*

There was a knock at my door and I looked up to find Luke.

"Hey," he said.

"Hey, everyone's gone for the day?" I asked.

"Yep."

"Great, come in. What did you find out?"

Luke took the seat on the opposite side of my desk. At this point, Luke was my only ally. It warmed me to see him. Being the cold, asshole boss at work made for a lonely life.

"It turns out Liam is flying back on Saturday," he started.

"Isn't that a little tight if he plans on attending the retirement party?"

"Yes. Perhaps he doesn't want to answer questions. He isn't flying back alone."

My ears perked. "How do you know?"

"He bought two first class tickets."

"Do we know the mystery companion?"

"No." He snorted. "I'm good but not that good, Nick. I'm not law enforcement. I assume a female companion."

"That would explain the lack of contact with Ms. Agostini," I said as I rubbed my chin.

"Yeah, I don't quite understand that situation. Gina told me that he kissed Ava right before he left and asked her to wait for him. But both Ava and Gina claim he hasn't called her. I'm not sure what his plan is but they land Saturday so I'm sure they'll both be at the retirement party."

Yes, my father's retirement party. It will probably, no correction, it will be an obnoxiously over the top affair that I am sure my stepmother organized detail by detail. Damn how that woman loved to throw a party, all so she could flaunt her wealth. The worst of it was that my father allowed it. On all accounts, he had never been one to flaunt his wealth or name while my mother was alive.

This situation with Liam had me concerned. I could be making something out of nothing. But when you are promoted to CEO of a family-owned business after fighting tooth and nail for it against your brother, then said brother disappears for weeks without contact, it brings up questions of loyalty.

Especially now that I was met with resistance with our current acquisition. Liam clearly didn't accept my promotion lightly. Now, I couldn't help but wonder if Laurent was pulling out of the deal because of Liam.

I stood up to stretch my legs. As I walked to the windows, we both flinched as we heard a crash out in the hallway. My head jerked toward the door.

"I thought you said the place was clear, that everyone had gone home?"

"They did." Luke stood up and rushed to the door, opening it in one quick move. "Ava!" He exclaimed. "What are you doing here?"

Ava? What the hell was she doing at work? I walked to the door to find her on the floor, picking up papers and files. Her hair was in a ponytail and she was wearing sneakers with workout tights. She looked like a kid, petite, now that she wasn't in her usual high heels.

"Ms. Agostini?" I questioned. "What are you doing here? At the office? It's after 6:30, shouldn't you be home with your children?"

"Hi, Luke. Mr. Closter," she said, briefly looking up in my direction. "I came to pick up the Laurent file. I left it here and need to proofread it. In my rush, I knocked over the filing unit."

"You came all the way out here to pick up a file?" asked Luke, while shaking his head. He leaned down to help her with the wire filing unit and the multiple files on the floor. I stood stoically like a bystander watching their natural exchange, an exchange I seemed unable to have with Ms. Agostini. "Where are the kids?"

"The kids had soccer practice and we were grabbing a quick bite. I wasn't far from the office. They are in the parking lot. I know Mr. Closter doesn't like children, so I thought it best not to bring them in. I wouldn't want to get kiddie germs in here."

"Why does everyone assume I don't like children?" I questioned.

"Because you don't," smirked Luke.

"Right," stated Ava flatly. "So, they are with George."

"George?" I asked.

"The security guard. He's keeping an eye on them." She stood, holding the manila envelope in her hands. She smoothed her ponytail and I followed her movement with my eyes.

"Well, I have the file, so I'll be going. Luke, thank you for the help."

"Very well. I'll need that in my hands by 9:00 tomorrow morning," I said.

"Yes, I'm going to start working on it as soon as the kids are in bed. I'll email it to you tonight."

"Have a good night, Ms. Agostini."

"Good night," she said, looking at me briefly.

"Have a good night, Ava, call if you need us to watch the kids so you can finish that file. Wouldn't want the tyrant here to not get his files on time and THANK YOU," he said in an over exaggerated manner, looking in my direction.

"Thanks, no worries, it will get done," reassured Ava before turning to leave.

"Tyrant?" I questioned as I watched Ava get in the elevator. "Whatever!"

I walked back into my office, hurrying my steps toward the window. I looked out and waited for Ava to walk out toward her car. Sitting on a nearby bench was George, the presumed security guard, laughing and watching while two young kids ran around the parking lot in front of him. Ava stopped near George and the kids ran over and hugged her.

"By the way," I said as I watched them hug and kiss each other. My chest stiffened, hardening under a pressure that was becoming too prevalent. "It's not kids I don't like, Luke. I just don't want any of my own."

"I know. It just comes across that you don't like them." Luke sat down, crossing his leg over his knee and started fidgeting with his shoelace. "You know, on the topic of Ava, I'm going to tell you this because no one else will." He looked up in my direction as I walked back to my chair and plopped down exhausted with the day.

"Go on," I said, urging what I knew would be words I didn't want to hear.

"You've been a real asshole to her. Lighten up. She hasn't done anything to deserve it."

"I'm not mistreating her. I've let her keep her schedule."

"We both know the Laurent proposal does not need to be proofread for tomorrow morning."

"No but let's see how she does with it."

"She's been proving herself and she proved herself before you even got here. She continues to prove herself because she knows just as well that the file doesn't need to be finished tomorrow but she still came out here after hours with her kids in tow to get the file."

He had a point, all good valid points but I wasn't going to admit it.

"Yes, she was Liam's assistant and yes, they had a close relationship but that's all it was and she doesn't deserve to pay for your feud with him." I thought about his comment. I was being more of a brute to her than necessary.

"I'll try to lighten up as you say but it's my nature."

"Fix your nature. She doesn't deserve it or need it. She needs this job and you need her, although you may not think so."

"Assistants are a dime a dozen," I said flatly. "And a new hire would have no issue obliging to our work schedule."

"Is she worth the extra effort to find a replacement? I think you have enough on your plate."

He was right, yet again.

"Let's see how she does with the Laurent file and go from there."

"I don't understand." He played with his shoelace again, nodding his head and then his face lit up as if something occurred to him. he suddenly shot up. "I'll be damned!"

"What?" I asked.

"We never discussed your incident at the café with the woman who bumped into you with the coffee." A sly smile overtook his face. "That first day you were back. You said you knew the girl. You said she was familiar." He was staring at me, reading me, I was sure but I remained stoic. "It was Ava, for sure! Do you and she have some history or something? What's your deal with her? You have a vendetta against her?"

"What! Don't be ridiculous, Luke."

"Well, what other reason is there for you to want her out so bad?"

"We don't have history. She isn't who I thought." I staggered to the wet bar and poured myself a drink. "You want one?" I asked over my shoulder.

"No, I don't want a drink but I'm killing to know what your deal is."

"No deal Luke, just mistaken identity." I thought over my words, "Ms. Agostini and I do not know each other. There is no vendetta. So just drop it."

There was no vendetta, no issues, other than the fact she worked for my brother and I wanted to clean house of anyone cut from the same cloth as him. That was the reason and it should be reason enough.

Chapter 11
Nicholas

The next morning, I surprisingly awoke to an email from Ava with the proofread Laurent proposal. It was time stamped at 1:10 a.m. She didn't disappoint. She got it to me by 9:00, just as I had asked, and it was perfect. My reasons for disliking her were quickly disappearing.

I made a stop at Café Avignon for a coffee on my way to a meeting downtown and on my return to my car, I spotted Ava's car. She was parked two spots over. What was she doing just sitting in her car? I couldn't figure her out. She impressed me by sending me the proposal before the deadline then she disappointed me by being late to work.

I couldn't pretend to not see her. I was sure she must have already spotted my car. Damn this day! I reluctantly walked over to her car and knocked on her window. She jumped, startled and rested her hand on her chest as she proceeded to open her window.

"Ms. Agostini, what, please tell me, are you doing here sitting in your car in this parking lot at a quarter to 10. Shouldn't you be at work?" She turned to me, her face was wet with tears and her eyes were red.

"Mr. Closter, I'm sorry. It's my son's first day at his new preschool. It's across the street over there," she said, pointing. I looked across the street. I never noticed a preschool on this road and I pick up my coffee here every morning but there, clear across from us, was indeed a preschool.

Little Star Preschool and Enrichment Center. A cute little gray and white building with large windows and a fenced in playground.

"I can't leave until I know he is ok," she continued, her voice cracking as she cried.

"Why wouldn't he be alright?" I asked.

"He hasn't moved since I left him." Her cries turned to sobs. Her shoulders shook and her breathing was jagged. What the hell! I hated the sight of crying women. What was I to do? I couldn't just turn around and leave her. I pulled out my pocket square, handing it to her.

"Here take this." She eyed it and took it slowly into her hand before wiping her tears with it. "And take this," I said, handing her my new cup of coffee that I hadn't even tasted yet. I sighed, stretching my arm toward her, "You need it more than I do."

"I'm sorry, I am an emotional mess." She looked down at her lap and shook her head. "It's the lack of sleep. I was up late." That was a dig at me. Obviously, I knew she was up late because of me and the Laurent proposal.

She folded my pocket square neatly in her hands. "I can't take your coffee. I know how much you need it."

I smirked, "Ah yes, the ongoing joke that the boss can't be approached before he's had his cup of coffee. I know. I know exactly the rumors that go around at work. No worries, I have already had two today and I'll get another before I leave."

I looked around the parking lot and across the street to the playground. What the hell was I doing? I tapped on the car door. "Now unlock the passenger door. I'm coming in."

"Excuse me?" She asked, wide eyed with both surprise and confusion.

"Ms. Agostini, there are two situations going on here that I don't like; a child crying and a mother crying and I can't leave you like this. Lord knows I won't forgive myself if I do and I have enough keeping me up at night."

She unlocked the door and I went around to the passenger side. Getting in, I adjusted my jacket, undid the button, making myself comfortable. I returned my eyes to the playground across the way. A playground that was overrun with children. Boys and girls but they all looked the same to me.

"Ok, help me out, which child am I looking for? Which one is yours?"

"The little boy that isn't moving."

I scanned the playground. She could help me out and be a little more descriptive but as my eyes roamed, I didn't have much issue locating him as he was the only child not playing. "Black shorts, red shirt?" I asked.

She let out a cry and nodded. I watched the child for a short while. He was standing with his head down, looking at the pavement. He was clearly uninterested in the surrounding environment. "He isn't crying, that is a good sign. It looks like he is just taking in his surroundings. He is observing," I said. "I don't think you have anything to worry about."

"He looks sad," she said. "I need a sign, something to tell me he is ok and that this isn't a mistake. It was my choice to move him to this school because it is more convenient with pickups and drop offs with work." She swallowed a cry with her eyes closed and put her hand to her chest as she took a deep breath, a tear falling down her cheek. "Now I am sitting here, feeling selfish."

She took a sip of the coffee I gave her. She made the cutest scrunched-up face. "How do you drink this? Black, no sugar? It tastes like mud."

I laughed, taking in her cute expression. "That is a double espresso, Ms. Agostini. That is what keeps me running."

"Your poor heart!" She exclaimed. "You better slow it down with these and watch your ticker."

"Thank you, Ms. Agostini, for your concern. I have a physician and my ticker is just fine." Although that did get me thinking that perhaps she might have a point. I was drinking too much coffee and not eating, could that be the cause of my recent heart palpitations? I wondered if she had taken notice. Was she a better observer than I gave her credit?

I continued watching the child, her son, wondering what if anything would make her feel at ease so that we could both move on with our day. Then I watched as a small soccer ball bumped into his leg and he looked up. The first movement I had seen from him since I stepped into the car.

A little girl wearing a sunflower print dress with her hair in pigtails ran up to him. She was speaking to him. He looked up and he kicked the ball back to the little girl and then he ran off with her, both playing with the ball.

I hit my hand on my knee, overly excited. "There you go, Ms. Agostini!"

She smiled and laughed. "Oh! Thank God!"

"Smart boy you have! He ran off with the prettiest girl. That a boy!"

"Mr. Closter, he is 3 years old; I hardly think it matters it was a girl."

"Ms. Agostini, he's a boy, it matters. Regardless, it worked, he's off and playing."

She smiled and continued wiping her tears with my pocket square. She was beaming now. I felt like an ass for admitting this but right then at that moment, she looked stunning. She was glowing with relief and dewy from crying. I liked to see her smile. I liked to see her happy. I couldn't explain why but it made me happy.

"Ready to head into work now?" I asked.

"Yes, I feel much better. Thank goodness." She folded up my pocket square meticulously. "Thank you for sitting with me and thank you for the coffee." She returned my pocket square.

I nodded, "Keep it, Ms. Agostini. It appears you need it more than I do. Besides, I have at least another thirty at home." I fixed my tie and buttoned my jacket. "I have a meeting downtown. I should be back by 11:30. See you then?" She shook her head and I opened the door to step out.

"Mr. Closter?" She called after me. I turned back to look at her. "Thank you," she said with a smile.

"Don't mention it. Now go to work!" I commanded.

I returned to my car. I knew I told Ava I would get another coffee but I didn't have time now. She needed it more than me. I could make it through one meeting at the bank and get a coffee on the way back. My cell phone pinged with a text message. As I slowed at a red light, I pulled my phone out of my jacket pocket and read.

Ms. Agostini: *I noticed you did not go back into the café for another coffee. I will be sure to have a double espresso and your favorite panini upon your return. The least I can do. And thank you again, boss.*

I didn't know why but I found myself smiling. I didn't feel so bad about not getting a coffee now. It didn't feel like I needed it. Besides, I had a coffee and panini to look forward to later.

Chapter 12
Nicholas

Friday morning. The end of a very long, rollercoaster week. It was also the day before my dad's retirement party. A party I was not looking forward to. It was an event I would rather skip out on, except that I was the replacement and there would be many business associates attending, not to mention our employees.

It was yet another uncharacteristically hot as hell day. Shit, all these years living in Paris made me forget how hot Vilamor could be year-round. I felt like an ungrateful complainer. I should be thankful for the daily sunshine and perhaps if I was a teenager again, driving around in swim shorts, I would be but wearing suits and leather loafers in this heat made me grumpier than usual.

I invited Ava to lunch. I picked our usual location, Cafe Avignon. It was odd meeting her out of the office for lunch when we spent all morning together at the office but I thought getting her out of the office and in a relaxed environment might allow for more honesty.

I had received her background check and there were items I wanted to discuss. I would like to think I could trust her but her story had some holes that concerned me.

I felt torn. Somewhere, somehow, it felt that I was crossing the line and even as I sat there in the wrought iron chair waiting for her arrival, I continued questioning if I should proceed. I pulled out a cigarette and lit it, needing to take off the edge while I waited.

Smoking was a nasty habit I had picked up in Paris. Typically, I lit up after drinking or more truthfully after sex but lately, I'd been lighting up more often. Sex deprivation, stress, the chest pains, whatever the reasons.

I inhaled and then exhaled slowly, letting the smoke out as the nicotine worked its magic. A puff escaped my lips as I watched Ava's white Acura pull into a spot across from where I sat. My gaze lingered on her as she checked her hair and makeup in the rear-view mirror before getting out of the car. No need for impressions where I was concerned but I appreciated her effort.

She smiled when she saw me and let her head tip down as she took brisk steps toward me. The incident yesterday with her son at the preschool changed the dynamic between us. I hadn't spoken to her after my return, as I was bombarded with meetings and phone calls but she did seem to smile more than usual.

This morning was much the same. Her mood toward me this morning was different from the prior mornings as was mine toward her. Something about sharing that moment with her yesterday. Watching her as a mom, a protective mom, made me see her in a different light.

She walked in the direction of the café now with an energy about her that seemed to attract attention. She was met with friendly waves and greetings. People had clearly gotten to know her about town and she waved at many as she crossed the parking lot. She tucked a strand of hair behind her ear and smiled as she approached.

She had a grace that made her attractive and I couldn't peel my sight from her. She was so unaware of her beauty and her presence. Morally, I knew it wasn't appropriate but lately, my body was becoming a traitor whenever I was in her company.

I admired her dark hair pinned up. A few random strands framed her heart shaped face. She wore a pink blouse and it brought out the rosiness of her cheeks. I liked it. I liked how it made her look soft, almost angelic. And I briefly second guessed my intentions.

"You really should lay off those," she remarked from behind her chair as she pointed to my cigarette. "They are awful for your health. You should know better, Mr. Closter."

I placed the cigarette on the white saucer in front of me and smudged it, putting it out. I knew she hated it when I smoked, she hated all things unhealthy and unnatural. I had all intentions of putting it out when she got here anyway.

"Good afternoon." I motioned for her to take a seat. She pulled out her chair and sat.

"So, what can I do for you? Why this urgent meeting?" She asked as she placed her handbag on the chair to her left.

"Right to the point?" I questioned.

"Yes, it is 12:15 on a Friday, I have what is equivalent to a weeks' worth of work left to do by the end of the day today and I need to pick up my kids at 3:00. So, we need to get this little meeting underway."

I had been working her too hard. I could admit it and I could admit no one could complete the workload I had given her by the end of the day. I sat back in my chair, taking my time gathering my words and I watched her as she sat up, straightening her spine.

My eyes went to the V-neck of her blouse, a habit I had to stop. I caught myself before it became awkward. I dragged my palm down my face, dreading this. Here it went.

"Tell me about your husband." As soon as the words were out, her demeanor changed. I saw it in the rise of her cheeks, the way she sat up even straighter as the anger rose to the surface.

"You brought me here to talk about my husband?" She puffed her cheeks, letting out a slow exhale. "What is this? Is this your way of getting to know me? Inviting me for lunch during business hours to pry into my personal business?"

"Where's your husband, Ava?" I pressed as I asked again, ignoring her questions. Her lips pursed into a thin line.

"He's dead. He died in a car accident on the highway."

I crossed my leg over my knee. "Yes, that is what you tell everyone, isn't it? Where did he go, Ava?" I watched her. I studied her actions, her demeanor and her stillness. She didn't move, she didn't speak and I couldn't see her thoughts with those damn oversized sunglasses covering her eyes. I continued my interrogation, "I ran a background check on you."

"So, this is what it is? You invited me here to fire me? You could've done it in the office, it would have been easier." Her breathing was becoming more rapid. "Is that even legal? Can you just run a background check randomly on your employees?"

"You signed a release when you were hired. It's in your file. Everyone signs the release. All my employees have had background checks upon being hired. Brother dearest didn't run one on you. He is under the impression you are a widow too, isn't he? I wonder how things would be different if he had run your background check."

"Ok, I see where this is going." She extended her elegant hand toward me to shake my hand. "Mr. Closter, it's been a pleasure working for Closter

Enterprises. It has been the most rewarding and challenging experience in my life. I will pack my belongings and be sure to catch Gina up on where I stand with all my current projects."

I took her hand, but I didn't shake it. Instead, I leaned in, closer to the table as I took her hand in mine and pulled her forward with a gentle tug, bringing her closer to me with that one quick gesture. She inhaled a startled gasp, her face now mere inches from mine. We were within an intimate distance, a distance that bordered on improper given our relationship.

This close to her, I got a trace of her sweet scent that unknowingly invaded my senses. It was an aroma that I had gotten much too accustomed to over the past few weeks as it seemingly saturated into the very walls of my office. I no longer walked into Closter Enterprises without noticing that now identifiable scent. It was a faint scent of orange blossoms and something else uniquely Ava that was threading its way into all my new memories of Vilamor.

My eyes darted to her chest that was now rapidly rising and falling with her frantic breathing. She really did think I was firing her and I could only imagine the thoughts racing through her mind.

I stared back at her lips. Shiny, glossy and slightly parted pink lips. I let go of her hand, slowly resting it on the table. I hunched forward, placing my hands on either side of her sunglasses as I slowly pulled them from her face.

There she was. There were those eyes. Those eyes that so reminded me of my youth. Of my carefree summer days. Her eyes, the deep, dark chocolate eyes, they couldn't hide secrets. Those eyes didn't lie, they weren't capable of lying. She looked at me. She really looked at me, the way only she could. She blinked once and it finally brought me back to the here and now.

"Where is your husband?" I asked again. I wanted to see if she would tell the truth and how much she would share. I knew those eyes but the light they once emitted was gone and I realized I no longer knew this woman. She had secrets and I needed to know if she was a fraud.

This woman, Ava or Frankie? Was she a widow or a disgruntled separated wife? I needed to know because I didn't want to believe that the beautiful memories from my youth, the memories of a perfect and happiest of summers were fake and based on lies. So, I pushed on. She shook her head, not wanting to answer me but I pushed. "He isn't dead, is he Ava?"

Those glorious eyes turned glassy. She was on the verge of tears but she didn't look away, she didn't hide.

"He left. He is gone." She looked down to the table. "Overseas somewhere."

"Why does everyone say you are a widow? Why do you tell people he is dead?" Her lashes fluttered open as she looked back at me.

"Because it's easier." She leaned back in her chair. "It is easier to say that he was taken from me than to admit that he left. He had a choice and he chose to leave. My life is easier if he is dead, not just gone. It is easier for me to get up every day and live."

I leaned back in my chair. Shit. So, he left her. Left his kids.

"Are you satisfied?" She asked.

I was pleased that she had been honest but I wasn't satisfied with the truth. I didn't feel good about the truth. I didn't like the truth. I would prefer he'd be dead too. And now as I watched her, exposed by the admittance with tears glistening on her cheeks, I had an overwhelming feeling of guilt that I brought on those tears.

"For future reference," she said, wiping a tear, "this was none of your business. My home life has nothing to do with my work ethic or performance. You know nothing about me, yet felt you had the right to pry into my personal life. I don't talk about it, not even to my own family. You may be my boss and I should have nothing but respect for you but sadly I can't say that."

"You, Nicholas Closter, have been a sadistic jerk and I still show up to work every day because I need the job and I respect your father, your brother and I love the culture at Closter Enterprises. But don't ever get it confused or think it has anything to do with you." She yanked her purse from the seat it rested on and put her sunglasses back on.

"I assume we are done here. Like I said, I have a lot of work, so I'll see you back at the office." She stood up, pulled in her chair and walked toward her car.

I remained seated, feeling like the complete sadistic jerk as she had just called me. Luke was right, it wasn't fair to run the background check. Not at this point. She had put in months of hard work. Maybe I was doing this for myself as opposed to the company. I was questioning my own intentions.

There was so much unsaid between us. She didn't talk about our past, not even mentioning it in passing. She was hiding something. There was a story to be told. Now I wished I had just allowed time to take its course.

Chapter 13
Nicholas

That afternoon, I finally got around to reading the Laurent proposal that Ava put together. The guilt ate at me as I reviewed it. The more I read the deeper my wrongdoing became. Luke was right, Ava was good, and I perhaps ruined forever what could have been a very good working relationship.

I gathered the file and my keys. I had to pick up my tux for tomorrow. I was going to have Ava do it but I was avoiding her since I had returned from our lunch meeting. I was headed out when I heard what sounded like crying from around the corner.

It was coming from the area around Gina's desk. Luke had mentioned how sensitive and emotional she was lately. I was not good at comforting crying women and not in the mood to deal with her. I was considering going around the long way. Then I heard Gina's voice. She wasn't crying, she was fine, she was the one comforting, so who was she comforting? Who was crying?

"I'm just tired, Gina. I'm burned out. This is hard and I don't just mean the job. It's all of it, the job, the kids and the house, all of it. I'm tired, I'm burned out and I don't know what to do."

"You have a right to feel that way. You haven't had a break since moving back and God only knows how much longer before that."

It was Ava, those were Ava's sobs. Why was she crying?

"What has happened? What is making you feel this way?" asked Gina.

"This, just all of this. I was up until almost 2:00 proofing the Laurent file."

"Why? That is so not necessary," said Gina.

"Yeah, I know, tell me about it. He, who shall remain nameless, wanted it by 9:00 this morning. That's fine but with everything else he's had me do this week, I didn't get around to it and had to take it home."

"He really said it was due at 9:00 when he knows you don't even start your day until 9:30?"

"Yep! Oh Gina, he's been horrible. He invited me to lunch today to confront me about my marital status. He ran a background check and obviously I am married, not widowed. Like it is any of his business! And I don't want to be that person whose husband left."

"I know, I know," said Gina, comforting her.

"He thinks he is almighty. So, was that his way of making me feel like crap? Or putting me in my place? I just don't think it's going to work out for me here. Not with him."

"Don't say that. Ava, you need this job, you love it here."

"Loved. I loved it here. Past tense. These last few weeks have been miserable. You know it. Don't try to say you haven't seen it."

"Oh, we have all seen it! Luke has talked to him about it. I thought that would help. I guess not."

"It's just a different environment now. Different administration and I don't think I fit the mold anymore."

She was unhappy, I knew that but now she was talking about quitting. This was exactly what I wanted but why did it not feel right? Why did this all feel wrong? I wanted her out, I wanted to push her out. Now I just felt like the tyrant as Luke called me. Maybe he was right, I needed Ava. Just as much as Ava needed the job.

With her possibly leaving me, I realized interviewing for a new assistant was the last thing I wanted to do a month after taking on this position. But now what? How do I mend this? We started off on this foot and I wasn't quite sure how to change the dynamic.

"Listen, dry those tears. Let's not have this talk here, ok?" suggested Gina. "This is why I called you over. I brought the dress."

"Oh, that's beautiful, Gina!"

"I think it will look great on you!"

"I don't know if it will fit."

"It should. I don't see why not, we've always shared clothes."

"Yeah, like how long ago? Before I had kids!"

"Well, if it doesn't fit, I can bring others when we pick you up."

"Yeah, I don't know, Gina. I don't know if I want to go."

"Oh, come on!" Urged Gina. "You have to! You haven't done anything fun for yourself since you've moved here."

"I'm tired, Gina. It's been a long week and I didn't get much sleep and I don't know if it's in me to be social at this point."

Now I felt like a real jerk. I have put so much on her that she was considering not going tomorrow. Why was I being so hard on her? This guilt was a heavy feeling.

"Come on! You have to go! Everyone from work will be there. You are still Nicholas Closter's assistant, regardless of how you feel for him. Besides, Liam will be there."

"Yes, that is really the only reason I am going," responded Ava.

And there it was. The motive for getting rid of Ava. My guilty disposition turned to anger. She was Liam's friend, assistant and potential love interest. I couldn't have that here, especially after he stormed in my office telling me he was going to take me down. I headed in the opposite direction, deciding to take the stairs so I wouldn't have to face her. I'd deal with all this after my father's party.

Chapter 14
Ava

I sat with an uneasy mood in the back of Luke's car, on the way to Mr. Closter's retirement party. Luke and Gina were making conversation in the front seats but I had zoned them out long ago. I was too nervous to partake in their small talk.

I was jittery with tension that magnified as we approached the Closter family neighborhood. The Closter's certainly knew how to throw a party, that was indisputable and I questioned my attendance as I took in the grandeur of the evening.

This was my first time to the Closter's home. I forgot how beautiful it was in the hills of Vilamor. It brought back fond memories of my youth. The butterflies in my stomach grew more unruly as we drove through a Cyprus tree lined driveway until we reached the beige stucco home, trimmed in white. It revealed itself at the top of a hill majestically and romantically tucked back out of the view of prying eyes.

I stepped out of the car onto the pavement. My chest squeezed with emotion as I took in the expansive views of Vilamor. The surrounding vineyards, groves and the sea beyond were thoroughly enjoyable from here. I closed my eyes and inhaled.

It truly was beautiful and being up here reminded me of the nights I would sit outside my grandmother's house and paint mental pictures of the future I wanted to have. I missed those days. I missed that girl. I missed the joy and anticipation I felt back then for my future. None of what I had dreamed for had come to fruition and being here was a painful realization.

I pushed those thoughts away and concentrated on tonight. The Closter home stretched before me, looking more like a high-end catering establishment than a multimillion-dollar house in the hills. The driveway was lined with bright white lights and a fountain in the center with a statue of Poseidon, an homage to Nicholas' Greek ancestry.

Just beyond the valet area were three wide stone steps, leading to a double wide front door open back to welcome the guests. Once in the marble foyer, we were greeted by servers wearing short dresses made of white feathers. They carried gold trays with clear, crystal champagne flutes, the bubbles in the gold liquid shined like diamonds from the light cast from the overhead strobe lights.

I swiftly grabbed a flute, opting to down the champagne instead of sipping it. I needed the courage after the stressful and awkward week. I was a wound-up mess, not to mention my heart was beating through my body like the bass of a drum. I was in no mood to face Nicholas Closter, which here, I knew would be inevitable.

The nerves and anger I had toward him, mixed with the anxious excitement of seeing Liam, was more than I could handle on an empty stomach. I needed the champagne and perhaps a few more to keep me here because I was close to bailing.

Gina turned her attention my way and grabbed my arm. "Hey there, you didn't waste any time finding the alcohol! Slow it down, I don't want to carry you home."

"You won't. No worries. I just need to loosen up a bit and get out of my head."

Luke held Gina's hand and weaved us through the crowds of people. And what gorgeous people they were! So many gorgeous people in one room. As I looked around, I spotted a few recognizable socialites mingling with the Closter family, friends and community. I let my eyes take in all the beautiful splendor of the party.

We strolled into a large room with French doors leading to a wraparound terrace. Above us, sparkling, crystal chandeliers hung from 20-foot ceilings. The room was an oasis of white; white hydrangeas and orchids hanging from doorways, vases, over white clad tables and throughout the stark white dance floor. The clean, bright white screamed of wealth and power.

"This room is gorgeous!" I whispered to Gina.

"Isn't it great!" She answered, leaning in. "Who even has a ballroom in their home anymore?"

I stood at one of the many white high-top cocktail tables beside Gina and Luke. I anxiously searched the room for Liam but there was no sign of him and my eyes settled back on Gina and Luke.

The farther along Gina got in her pregnancy, the more protective Luke became. It was cute and a twang of envy washed over me as I watched how protectively he kept his hand on her lower back. My husband had never been that way toward me and I had never felt as lonely in my marriage as I did during my first pregnancy. How sweet that Gina was being showered with so much dotting love and support.

The knot in my chest was growing bigger but I wouldn't allow myself to cry tonight or feel bad for myself. I looked around, searching for another tray of champagne. I tugged on my dress, realizing that oddly I matched tonight's theme. The gold sparkly dress reminiscent of the gold accents around the room.

I felt incredibly uncomfortable in my gown or should I say Gina's gown. It wasn't quite my style. I couldn't afford a gown on such short notice and this one was too gold, too sparkly, too low cut and the slit was a little too high for my liking.

To summarize, it was just 'too much'. I ran my hand down the side, pulling it in an unconscious effort to mysteriously expand the fabric. One could hope.

"Stop fidgeting!" exclaimed Gina, elbowing me in the ribs.

"Ava, you look terrific!" Luke added, catching onto the conversation.

"Thanks, it's your wife's gown."

"It never looked that good on me, you can keep it. I can't wear it now that you've made an appearance in it anyway. I don't even know if I'll ever fit in it again," she said, rubbing her hand on her belly.

"You look gorgeous too, babe." Luke brushed a kiss on her temple. "Ladies, I'm going to the bar, anything to drink?"

"Just get me a cranberry juice, honey," said Gina.

"Ok and for you, Ava?"

"I'll do another champagne. Might as well stick with what I have started."

"Ok, I'll go get those." My eyes followed him in the direction of the long, white acrylic bar where four male bartenders juggled to serve the guests.

"Why are you so fidgety today? And why are you so distracted?" Gina looked annoyed. It occurred to me that perhaps she had been trying to get my attention for a while.

"What do you mean? I just don't wear clothes like this anymore. I haven't dressed up in years. I'm uncomfortable. You know I don't like how I look and I can't even remember the last time I wore a gown, a strapless bra or got my hair done. It just feels strange."

"You look great. Most would die for that dress and you wear it well. The old Ava would live for something like this."

"It's not my style Gina, it's your style. I'm not that person anymore. I'm a mom."

"It used to be your style and this new style of yours isn't working for you, so you need some help. You know Ava, just because you're a mom doesn't mean you can't have fun. It's ok to do both." She looked throughout the room and huffed, "And why do you keep looking around?"

"I'm not."

"Yes, you are! You're looking for him, aren't you?"

"Who?" I asked, pretending I didn't know who she was referring to.

"You know who! Liam!"

"He's been gone for weeks. Just eager to hear how his trip went."

"Uh-huh, yep!" She said, tapping her fingers on the table. "When are you both going to stop with this silly charade and just admit you're into each other?"

"Gina, it's not like that. We are good friends and we have a great working relationship. I just need him to get me my old job back. I don't even know if he is aware that I'm not reporting to him anymore. I want to tell him before he gets to work on Monday."

"I'm also dying to tell him that his brother is indeed an ass and I don't know how he did it, growing up in the shadow of that man. He is an absolute pompous, arrogant, egotistical prick on a power trip."

And as my luck would have it, at that moment, Luke showed up with two drinks in hand; a red wine and a cranberry juice. Just behind him stood none other than Nicholas Closter, holding a flute of champagne. Dear God, did he hear what I said?

Did he know I was talking about him? I glanced his way and the sly smirk on his face said it all. He did indeed hear and no doubt knew it was in reference to him. He came to stand at my side, holding what I gathered was my champagne.

"Look who I met up at the bar!" Luke said in an overly excited tone as he handed Gina her cranberry juice. "This good man here," he said, pointing to Nicholas, "offered to help with our drinks."

"Good evening, ladies. Gina, you're glowing!" Nicholas bent his head to give her a peck on the cheek.

"Nah, it's just a hot flash." She winked with a smile.

"She's not kidding," said Luke. "Ava and I can both confirm the air conditioner was on full blast in the car the whole way here."

Gina laughed, "How are you, Nick?"

"I'm well," he turned his attention to me. "Ms. Agostini, your champagne." He extended his arm, handing me the glass. The smile he had for Gina was nowhere to be seen now. Pretentious ass. I already knew he didn't like me but he didn't need to make it so obvious to everyone else.

"Hello, Mr. Closter," I said dryly.

"You look lovely," he said, bowing his head while raking his eyes from my head to my toes, leaving goose bumps in their path.

"Same," I said flatly, giving his tux a quick look.

He looked good. He looked really good but the problem with men like Nicholas Closter was that he knew he looked good. He was hot and he knew it and I wasn't about to let him know that I thought so too. Too bad his personality and overall demeanor weren't as hot.

I looked back toward the center of the ballroom, my eyes continuing to scan for Liam. Oh Liam, where are you? Nicholas was standing close, too close. Didn't he have other people to go bother? Wasn't he supposed to mingle about and greet the other guests?

It took enough out of me to put up with him during work hours, must he bother me during non-work hours? I could feel his aura penetrating my personal space and it was frustrating. Hadn't he disturbed me enough this week?

He cleared his throat. "You like to dance, Ms. Agostini?"

"Not really. I'm not much of a dancer," I answered.

"Oh yes, she does!" Exclaimed Gina. I gave her wide devil eyes. What the hell was she doing?

"Ava loves to dance! In college, she was the first on the dance floor and the last to leave." Gina laughed and I despised her at that moment.

Nicholas nodded, amused as he listened to Gina's confession of our party days. "Maybe later, I can take you for a spin around the dance floor." I didn't appreciate his tone. His authoritative nature came across in a manner that told me he wasn't asking me to dance but rather telling me that we would.

Was I supposed to jump up and down, grateful that Mr. Closter was going to make room for me on his dance card? Spare me, not interested.

"That won't be necessary," I said, continuing to look ahead at the dance floor, avoiding Nicholas Closter's eyes. "It's hardly professional for you to be dancing with your assistant."

"I don't see why not. I've danced with Gina throughout the years."

"She's your cousin's wife and was never your assistant."

"Be nice!" Gina whispered in my ear.

"I am being nice."

He smiled with a slanted brow and bowed his head in our direction. "Excuse me, ladies." He turned to leave just as a clanking of silverware was heard against a glass. Silence slowly began to fall among the party goers and I turned my attention back toward the dance floor in the direction of the clanking.

There in the center of the white dance floor stood Mr. Closter, holding a microphone. Mrs. Closter stood to his right, followed by Liam and a beautiful blonde woman. I studied the blond. Beautiful didn't even begin to describe her. She had the shiniest, pin straight hair that fell to her mid back and she wore a red gown.

Liam stood next to her at a rather close distance. He held a champagne glass in one hand and his other hand was in his pocket. He looked good. He looked different. Mr. Closter cleared his throat to speak, the microphone crackling with static.

"Thank you all for coming. My wife and I want to extend a warm welcome. This evening is not only a farewell but a thank you for serving and being a part of the Closter Enterprise family. Every one of you has played an important part in our success."

"I am taking a step back but have all the faith in our sons, Nicholas and Liam. We know that with you all by their side, Closter Enterprises will continue to succeed and dominate in the luxury liquor industry."

Mr. Closter tilted his champagne glass my way. The eyes of hundreds of guests flowed in my direction and I became aware the glances were for

Nicholas who remained at my side. I turned my head as I now noticed his presence at my right. He hadn't gone very far after all. Nicholas tilted his head toward his father in acknowledgement.

The crowd of guests applauded but to my right, I felt only a tense, aggressive vibe radiating from Nicholas. I watched him from the corner of my eye. He didn't applaud, nor did he look overly enthusiastic about any part of the evening thus far.

This was about him and him taking over as CEO, following in his father's footsteps. He should be overjoyed but Nicholas's body language said something different. Was this not what he wanted?

Mr. Closter walked closer to Liam and put his hand on his shoulder. I heard an extended sigh coming from my right and I turned my head slightly to where Nicholas stood.

He held his glass so tightly, his knuckles were turning white. Mr. Closter could fool anyone with his little speech, making it appear that the Closter's were a united front but as I studied Nicholas Closter, I found myself questioning their relationship and it occurred to me that not everything was well in the Closter family.

As I thought about it more, I found it odd that Nicholas wasn't standing with his family on the dance floor? He was the new CEO after all. But for whatever unknown reason, he chose to not be, nor did Mr. Closter invite him to join.

"Speaking of my son. This is as good a time as any to announce that my wife and I are overjoyed at the recent engagement of our son, Liam to Samantha Laurent." The crowd applauded and gasps of cheers and congratulations were heard. I saw camera flashes as the beautiful blond draped her two arms around Liam, pulling him in for a kiss.

Wait, what! Backup. What did Mr. Closter just say? Did he say Liam was engaged? That couldn't be. I watched as Liam put his arm around the beautiful blond and laid a kiss on her lips. The beautiful blond picked up her left hand and pointed it outward toward the crowd, showing off her large, sparkly diamond ring.

Oh my God! What was going on? Was this a joke? Just a few weeks ago, Liam had kissed me. Those lips had been on my lips. I looked at Gina, she looked as surprised as I felt. She shook her head at me, answering the question that I hadn't yet asked.

"Did you know?" she asked, turning to Luke.

"No, no, I had no idea. I didn't even know they were dating. They've hung out but Samantha's just like that—"

He kept talking but I wasn't listening anymore. I felt a warmth ripple through my body. My ears were ringing and my mouth went dry with a nauseous feeling. I leaned on the cocktail table for support.

How could it be? How could he be engaged? He wasn't even dating anyone, right? He never mentioned her or any woman for that matter. How could we have been so close, yet I never even heard about this Samantha.

And he kissed me. He kissed me before he left and as much as I hadn't mentioned it, there was more to that kiss. He wanted more. I know it. After all, he asked me to wait. Gina and Luke were still talking about Samantha. I didn't give a shit about this Samantha. I just wanted to know why Liam never mentioned her.

My mouth watered with the all too familiar sour taste of nausea. It was taking over and I needed to get out of there soon. I closed my eyes to keep the tears away, to erase all the feelings out of my system before they cascaded out. I didn't understand why I was reacting this way. I'd done this before. I had worked through rejection when my husband left and I could do it again. Just breathe in and out and repeat.

My body reacted with a shiver when a smooth, warm hand rested upon my forearm. I twitched, startled when an equally warm, soothing voice appeared at my ear. "Ms. Agostini, I believe it is time for that dance."

I opened my eyes with recognition, turning in the direction of the voice. Nicholas was there. He was still there. He hadn't left. He took the champagne glass from my hand, placing it on the table. I shook my head to tell him no. I just couldn't. I couldn't dance right now; I couldn't act normal.

And I couldn't face Liam, not yet. Nicholas leaned over. His face was so close to mine that I could smell his aftershave, a mixed scent of bergamot and teakwood that was quickly making me dizzy.

"Come on. You look like you need this." For the first time, I saw something resembling kindness in his eyes. "Take my hand and come with me." He urged.

At that moment, Nicholas Closter understood me. He understood my feelings almost as if he was going through them too. I could feel that he needed this as much as I needed it. I don't know why but I felt it in my core. I nodded and gave him my hand as he turned and guided me toward the dance floor. My legs took over.

I walked behind him, holding his hand as we weaved through tables and guests. I was aware of the eyes on me. The eyes on us. Why wouldn't they be looking? He was the new CEO and I, his assistant.

Nicholas took me to the center of the dance floor and turned toward me, taking me in his arms. His body was hot with a comforting heat that wrapped around me like a blanket. But his face and his frame were so close, it was unnerving. Could he tell I was uncomfortable?

"You're shaking," he said, confirming my suspicions. "Just relax."

I looked into his eyes. This close, they looked like kaleidoscopes. They were too close, in fact. The hairs on the back of my neck saluted as we connected. I hated this man, right? I should hate him but at that moment, I didn't. Who was this sweet man? Was this my grumpy boss?

He was being uncharacteristically nice to me. Was he coming to save the day as he had so many years ago? I blinked those thoughts out of my mind, burying them deep into my past as I had all this time.

"Why are you so uncomfortable?" He asked but I didn't answer. There wasn't much I could say that would allow for a comfortable Monday morning at work, so I let the question hang as I watched the other couples and took in the details of the room.

"Tell me about your kids," he asked, changing the subject. "Where are they today?"

A topic I could talk about. One that wouldn't make our relationship awkward. Keep it professional, I reminded myself. "My landlady, she lives next door. She came over to do dinner and bedtime."

"That's convenient that you have that. Do you use her often, for babysitting?"

I continued, disinterested and looking everywhere except at Nicholas Closter. "No, not at all. I don't want to take advantage of it. She's elderly and it's too much for her."

Why were we having this conversation? Why did he care? He hadn't cared. In all the weeks of working together, he had never asked me anything about my kids.

Nicholas bowed his head, leaning closer into my personal space. His warm breath was at my neck, making my skin tingle. He took an obvious, exaggerated inhale, feeling as if he was consuming me in. I couldn't explain it but he stole my breath with his inhale and I was suffocating. My heart was beating heavier than the percussion and I was fading fast.

"I want to apologize about yesterday," he whispered into my ear. "I caught you off guard and clearly in hindsight, I crossed the line." He tugged me closer still, his hand pressing on my mid back. "Please accept my apology."

I gave in, finally turning my face as our eyes locked. The connection was electric. It crackled like a fourth of July sparkler and I forgot myself and who he was. The song ended and another started. It was just enough to get me out of the haze.

"I need some air. Excuse me." I turned and quickly left the ballroom, going somewhere, anywhere where I could breathe. I just needed air.

Chapter 15
Nicholas

I stood in the center of the marble dance floor, watching as Ava ran off. Well, that was not what I was looking to accomplish. Had she run off because she despised me as much as I believed she did? Or did she run off because she felt what I felt?

It was there. That feeling was there. It had been there every day, every time but tonight, I didn't hide it. I didn't cover it up by being a cold shithead as I had before. Instead, I allowed myself to feel the feelings and let them guide me.

I don't know what it was about this evening but I couldn't avoid it anymore. The issue was that she wasn't ready for the feelings or the change in my demeanor.

What a messed-up night it was turning out to be. My brother engaged to my ex and me screwing things up with my assistant. I needed a drink, a hard drink and I needed a smoke. I headed in the direction of my father's study, knowing he'd have both the scotch and the cigars.

I looked around, to my left and to my right, waiting for the hallway to clear as I opened his study door and walked in. I took a seat at my dad's oak desk, pulling forward the silver-plated box that contained his Cuban cigars. I picked one out and brought it close, taking a deep breath inhaling the aroma.

That was when I heard the talking, unmistakably my stepmother's voice. What was Kate going on about now? Her voice was nails to a chalkboard, it was shrill and cold. I closed the cigar case and walked toward the French doors, taking care to not make any noise.

"Nice to meet you," responded the other voice, a voice I knew well. It was Ava.

"So, you are the infamous Ava?" Asked Kate, her voice dripping in mockery.

"Hardly infamous, Mrs. Closter."

"Don't be so humble. You are very pretty, after all. You've captured my son's attention for months now."

"Your son?"

"Yes, Liam. You've held his attention for quite some time. He would rant on and on about you. I was getting worried but luckily, he has moved on and found love with Samantha. You understand, don't you? Samantha is young, unattached, educated and well-bred. She has her whole life ahead of her. And you, you're—"

"Mrs. Closter, I assure you, you do not need to go on or be concerned."

"I know I don't because if you interfere, I will make your life in Vilamor impossible."

Typical Kate, threatening and dictating her son's life. I rolled my eyes as I heard her practiced speech. I could only imagine how many times and to how many girls she had said those exact words. Liam never had a girlfriend that stuck around for very long, presumably because none were good enough for Mommy dearest.

I had never seen her in action but damn, she was callous and calculating. I knew exactly what I needed to do and I was so happy to do it. I stuffed the cigar in my jacket pocket for later and moved the curtain aside as I stepped onto the terrace.

"Ava!" I said, overly enthusiastic. "There you are! I've been looking for you." I came behind Ava, wrapping my arm around her waist and placing a kiss on her temple. I was laying it on thick, which was confirmed when Ava looked up at me, with her confused, questioning eyes. "I came to gather you for some food."

"Nicholas?" Questioned Kate as she shifted her weight from one foot to the other.

"Kate, have you met my date, Ava?"

"Your date?" She examined Ava from head to toe with hostile eyes. "I didn't think you brought a date. I didn't think you were seeing anyone. You've only just returned to Vilamor."

"You know me, Kate! I'm never alone for long."

"I see. Well, I thought Ava was your assistant?"

"Hmm, yes, she is but what can I say, we go way back and she's captured my attention. She has that effect, doesn't she?" I threw Kate's words right back at her with a wink. "I'm sure you'll be as caring and generous with Ava as you have been with Samantha. After all, you know just how protective I am over things that are mine."

Kate's taut face turned red. With all her plastic surgery and fillers, I couldn't tell if she was surprised, frustrated or angry. I hoped it was all three. I felt Ava tense under my grip. I redirected my attention to her.

"Ava, have you met my dear stepmom, Kate?" Ava and Kate both remained silent but Ava nodded. "Well Kate, this has been a lovely conversation as always but my date is starving and I'm craving some alone time with her, so you'll excuse us." I tipped my head in Kate's direction.

"Ava, shall we?" I lent her my arm and after brief hesitation, she linked her arm through mine.

"Yes, let's."

Kate huffed and turned to leave, as did we. I took Ava back into the study and closed the French doors behind us to prevent eavesdropping.

"Mr. Closter!" exclaimed Ava with a note of embarrassment and what even sounded like relief, "What are you doing here?"

"I came for a drink and heard you with Kate. It sounded like you needed some saving."

She sighed, her whole body deflating. "I don't think she likes me very much."

"No, it's not that. You are a threat to her. Or should I say a threat to the future she hopes for her son."

"She has Liam and me all wrong. We were never involved." Her tone was a sign of worry and embarrassment.

"Perhaps not but that isn't what the general public believes, is it? And clearly my dearest stepmother has that belief as well."

"Mr. Closter, it's not what you think, it wasn't like that between us." I fixated on her use of my last name to address me.

"Stop calling me that," I commanded with a timbre that was more aggressive than I intended.

"Mr. Closter?" She looked startled and confused. "That is your name," she said flatly.

"My father is Mr. Closter. Did you call my brother Mr. Closter? Ever?"

"No, never. He was Liam, always just Liam."

"Right. I would appreciate if you similarly called me by my name. We are beyond formalities," I said.

Her eyes were downcast, blocking me from reading her thoughts. "And yes, I believe you," I added, before walking over to the bar cart to pour two scotches.

"This evening is turning into a disaster." She took a seat on the walnut-colored leather couch, resting her head in her hands. "I need to go home. I need to find a way to get out of here without anyone noticing. I just want to cuddle my babies and hide under a blanket."

"You have a night out and you want to give it up?" I questioned.

"It isn't fun. This hasn't been fun. I don't fit in. This isn't for me. I feel lied to by Liam. And his mom thinks I am a hussy. And you—"

"And me?" I raised an eyebrow in question.

She didn't respond. I walked closer, handing her one of the glasses of scotch. "Here, drink this."

She shook her head. "I don't drink hard liquor."

"Drink it," I commanded, "you're shaking, look at your hands. Besides, how can you work for a liquor company and not drink?" She looked down at her hands that were folded neatly in her lap and then looked back up at me.

"Walk out with me," I suggested. "Forget Liam exists. Forget Kate's words. Pretend his engagement affects you in no way."

"How do I do that?"

"By enjoying yourself and letting others see that you are enjoying yourself."

"Why would you help me? Why do you care?"

"Let's just call it a peace treaty, ok? My way of asking for an apology." Her eyes looked dubious. "I am requesting a fresh start. I stereotypically judged you and you've proven to be anything except the opposite of what I thought. You are also the best assistant I have ever had but don't tell any of the prior assistants. I will deny it."

A pink hue colored her cheeks as she smiled at the compliment. Her hand came up to meet mine as she took the glass tumbler and slowly lifted it to her lips. She tilted the glass back slightly and I watched as the amber liquid passed through her partly open lips. It was a small sip and she closed her eyes, while her face scrunched at the burn.

"Keep going," I urged, "you'll feel better in a while. Just give it time to kick in." She looked at me with bewildered eyes and brought the glass back up to her lips, taking a longer sip.

"That is awful," she cried.

I grinned at her reaction to the scotch. "Salut, Ava," I tapped my glass to hers with a wink. "Drink up!" I chuckled as I raised my glass to my lips, watching her do the same. Her eyes locked on mine as she took down the remaining liquid in one continuous gulp.

"That's awful, it really is," she said. "This is bad, this whole situation is bad. Should I quit?" she suggested, "I can't quit."

I smirked and stood up to go back toward the bar cart.

"Please don't quit, I just got started here. I don't really want to interview and look for another assistant. Just relax," I suggested.

"That's easy for you to say. I understand now why your father was never fond of me. He probably thought I was sleeping with his son. Can you imagine? And all the while, he had Samantha. How do I face everyone?"

I poured another round. "How? You are going to fix yourself; you're going to put on a smile and you're going to walk out those doors and have a good time. That's what you are going to do. Here, drink another." She took it down and looked up at me with those big doe eyes of hers.

I don't know what came over me but I wanted to cradle her and tell her this would all work out. My chest hurt with a sudden pressure that had been foreign until recent weeks.

I downed my drink before standing to full height and putting out my hand toward her. It didn't take much convincing. She took my hand and I gave her a reassuring squeeze. She stood up and we were now face to face, her brown eyes looking right up at mine.

I'm not sure why she was trusting me but I could see her soften. I felt at that moment that she was laying her stress, her anxiety, her uncertainty onto me and I couldn't fail her, not tonight.

I patted her hand, "You ready to do this?" I asked.

"As ready as I'll ever be."

Chapter 16
Nicholas

For the next two hours we danced, drank, laughed and ate. I came to the party solo but wasn't solo anymore. For all intent and purposes, Ava was my date tonight. It hadn't started that way but destiny had other plans. For anyone watching, it looked like we came together. I didn't mind it either. At least twice, I caught Samantha watching us and Liam wasn't far behind.

We stood outside on the terrace. Below us were the many lights of the city that shone bright with the sea just beyond. I was leaning against the white stone banister on the quiet end of the terrace, enjoying the breeze and the company. Gina and Luke left the stifling ballroom to join us for some fresh air.

Ava had convinced Luke to share stories of our childhood and Luke was much too enthusiastic to share. He was telling the story about the time he and I snuck out to go to a club and got a flat tire, which forced me to call home because neither of us knew how to change a tire at 16 years old.

I watched as Ava laughed and smiled, so carefree. I occasionally caught her looking my way or giving me a side glance. She was letting her guard down. Slowly, she was relaxing. Her rough edges were being sanded down and it looked good on her. She took her armor off and I guess I was taking mine off too.

Tonight was the first time I didn't purposely act cold toward her. I didn't think after tonight I could go back to playing that role and I didn't want to. I sure hoped she didn't clam up again after tonight. Although I was very aware that she was under the influence of too much alcohol.

"One more shot, one more shot!" Luke chanted.

"Not for me," I said with a nod.

"Clearly none for me," said Gina, rubbing her rounded belly.

"Ava? Ava, can I count on you? Will you do a shot?" He held his hands together like he was praying.

"I really shouldn't. Three champagnes and two scotches. Sorry, count me out too."

"You guys are all light weights! Ok, I tried, maybe at the engagement party?" We all looked at him, questioning. "Christopher and Alana's engagement party."

Oh yes, Luke's little brother was getting married and his engagement party was next week.

"I don't think I can go to Chris's party," stated Ava flatly.

"What!" Exclaimed Gina.

"Ava, why not? You have to come. My mom's counting you in. It's family."

"I know but I was supposed to go with Liam and well clearly that won't be happening. And I don't know how I feel about asking Mrs. Santos to watch the kids' back-to-back weekends."

"Just promise me you'll think about it and reconsider. My mom will be so disappointed."

"Your parents are so good to me. I'll think about it but I can't make any promises."

"Well then we can wait until Liam and Samantha's engagement party." We all looked at Luke like he had two heads. "Come on, you know Liam's mom won't leave behind an opportunity for a party." He had a good point. "Rain check for all except my wife but you need to make it up to me and tell me the story of how you two met."

Luke was pointing between Ava and me. I glanced to my side, smirking at Ava. The moment of truth. Did she remember me? Would she admit to knowing me? Would she tell the story of two teenagers meeting or would she tell the story of the run in outside the café? We had never spoken of either situation.

Ava stared at me with a smile on her lips. The tiny gleaming lights that hung over the terrace sparkled in her eyes, making them even more beautiful than they already were. The way the lights hit her eyes made me forget my train of thought.

"Well," she dragged the word out as she started, "it was the summer I turned 16." She stared at me with her dazzling smile and just like that my whole body let out an exhale that I hadn't even been aware I was holding. She did remember.

"I spent my summers at my grandparent's vineyard. I loved my summers there but every day without fail, my grandmother would take a nap in the afternoon. I would get so bored!" Her eyes twinkled as she told the story. "So, one day, it was a Tuesday, I remember. I went out to explore."

"My grandmother was always cautious and never wanted me to venture without her. Rightfully so, the property was beautiful but it had been years since my grandfather passed and the property needed repairs. In fact, we didn't even bother to harvest the grapes anymore."

"That day I waited for my grandmother to go take her nap and I walked to the end of the vineyard, to the cliff. I just wanted to get a better view. It was so far up, that from that perspective it felt like the sea was closer, almost like I could stretch out my arm, reach out and touch it." She held her hand out like she was there in that moment.

"I was standing on the edge and the stones from the retaining wall started to give out. I slipped and there I was, hanging. I was holding on to the edge but really it was a nearby branch that held me in place. It had caught onto my pocket and belt strap. I was so scared. I had never been that scared. I didn't know what to do. I had no upper body strength and the soil beneath my feet was crumbling."

Gina's hand went to her mouth, "Oh my God! Ava, you never told me. Nana Maria's house?" Ava nodded yes to her question.

"I didn't tell anyone. I didn't even tell my grandmother. I didn't want my father to find out. My dad had been on my grandmother to repair the property. He even offered to pay for all the repairs. But it wasn't about the money, my grandmother just didn't want to change anything. She wanted it all to remain as it had when my grandfather was still alive."

"So, what did you do?" asked Luke, bringing us back to the story. "How did you get up or down?"

Ava pointed to me with a smile. I nodded and returned a smile.

"Oh," Gina's eyes grew wide and she winked. "So, this is how it all started!" She clapped her hands together in excitement. "Tell the rest, come on, tell the rest! I'm dying to know the details."

I looked at Ava, her cheeks turning a pretty shade of pink. "You want to tell?" She asked me.

"Yeah, sure." I put my drink down on the banister and shoved my hands in my pockets. Let me get comfortable as I relived that day 22 years later. "So, like Ava said it was a Tuesday afternoon. It was a bright, cloudless, hot day. I was on my Vespa, heading to the beach."

"A Vespa?" Gina interrupted with a giggle.

"I was 19, Gina and it was the early 2000s. Vespas' were all the rage," I said with a smile.

"Ok, ok, point taken. I just can't picture you on a Vespa."

"Anyway, so I'm riding this Vespa down the back roads behind the vineyards and olive groves. I slowed down as I approached a bend and I see this girl hanging off the cliff. She was barefoot, her shoes had fallen off and her arms were stretched to the max."

"There was an olive branch hanging from the pocket of her jean shorts. Her dark wavy hair cascaded down her back and she wore a white tank top. And I thought holy shit, what the hell do I do?"

"What did you do?" asked Gina, fully engrossed in the story.

"The only thing any decent human being would do. I pulled over, got off the Vespa and went over to help her down."

I locked eyes with Ava. I relived it all just then. I relived the first time those same eyes locked with mine. They took my breath away then, that day at that moment and they had continued to every moment thereafter. Even today. Even now.

The adrenaline I had felt that day, was pumping through me now. My fingertips had sensory memory of the feel of her hips as I grabbed her to steady her. My hand that day had rested on her lower back, balancing her while I yanked and detangled the branch from her pocket. Her skin was warm and damp.

"What happened after you got her down?" asked Luke.

I cleared my throat, steadying my thoughts.

"He took me for a ride on his Vespa," Ava said, laughing, as she continued the story. "He took me to the beach. We went for a walk, got to know each other. He bought me an ice cream. Then took me back before my grandmother could worry about me." She laughed and tilted her head my way, her cheeks blushing again.

"So that's the story? Huh?" asked Luke, looking between Ava and me.

"Not quite. Every day thereafter for the rest of the summer, he would pick me up during my grandmother's nap and we'd take a Vespa ride."

"How romantic!" Gina said, her hand on her chest. "What happened after the summer?"

"Nothing," stated Ava flatly.

"Nothing!" Exclaimed Gina.

"I returned to college," I said. "I came back the following summer but the villa was abandoned. It was for sale. I tried to find her but I knew her as Frankie and she didn't return that summer."

"No, I never returned. My grandmother passed that winter. My father placed the villa for sale."

"Frankie?" asked Luke with a confused look.

"Yes, Ava was Frankie growing up," said Gina, laughing.

"Why?" asked Luke with a puzzled look on his face.

"My mother's name was Ava too. Couldn't have two Ava's in a household, so they called me by my middle name, Francesca, which by the age of three was shortened to just Frankie."

"When did you go back to Ava?" I asked.

"Um, shortly after my mom passed," she said, looking down toward her feet.

So, she was motherless too. I loved having things in common with her but I wished this wasn't one of them.

"Did you guys do the deed? My cousin must have tried to get in your pants." Of course, Luke would ask that question.

"Luke!" exclaimed Gina, lightly slapping her husband across the chest.

"Just a question between adults."

"No, never," laughed Ava.

"Never?" Luke's eyes were wide in disbelief.

"I am capable of being a gentleman," I said.

"Perhaps he didn't want too. Perhaps he wasn't interested." Ava sounded serious and melancholy as she smiled my way. Did she really believe I wasn't interested? I spent every day that summer from the beginning of July until the last week of August anxious for our two hours together but she seriously thought I wasn't interested in her. Delusional girl.

"I was." I nodded as I stared her straight in the eyes. "Every single day from that first day forward." Her cheeks grew rosy at my confession and I was very much satisfied with my admission and her reaction to it. Her vivid recount of our meeting proved to me that not only did she remember me and our time together but that it was as much a milestone in her life as it was in mine.

"Hmmm. It appears the ice-cold Nicholas Closter is secretly sentimental," joked Gina.

"You know, I don't understand how we didn't know each other growing up, how is it we weren't all friends?" asked Luke.

"Well, we are a few years apart in age and we grew up in different parts of town," stated Gina. "You and Nick grew up in the 'hills'," she said with air quotes, "and Ava and I are from the 'flats'."

Ah yes, the disparity between the socioeconomic areas of Vilamor.

"Yes but I met Frankie, should I say Ava," I corrected myself, "in the hills."

"I was at my grandmother's house that summer. My grandparents were in the hills but my dad married down and I grew up in the flats. I lived a block away from Gina until I was thirteen."

"What happened at thirteen?" I asked.

"That's the year Ava left me for New York," Gina said with sad puppy eyes and downward lips.

"Yeah, my dad took a new job and we relocated. I only came back in the summers."

A buzzing alarm sound went off and all four of us ceased as we looked around, searching for the sound. It was coming from Ava's purse.

"Oh!" she exclaimed, her eyes wide, as she opened the zipper of her clutch and took out her phone. "I have to go home."

"What?" Bellowed Gina. "What are you? Cinderella? What happens if you don't leave now?"

She chuckled. "No, I have to, really. I need to get back to the kids. Remember I told you about my landlady. I want to get home and relieve her. I set my alarm so I wouldn't be too late."

I looked at Gina then Luke and shrugged my shoulders. "Even on a night off at a party, she's organized."

"She always has been, that's why she's great at her job."

"Someone has to be," added Ava.

"You can't drive yourself home. You have had too much to drink," I stated.

"She came with us," said Luke, "I'll take you home, Ava."

"No, no, you're not doing that. You stay here with your wife. I'll get a ride from one of those rideshare drivers."

My chest tightened and my eyes went wide. "No, you're not, you aren't getting in a stranger's car in your condition and dressed like that." I pointed to her dress.

"What's wrong with what she's wearing?" asked Gina defensively.

"Nothing," I had lost count of the number of gawking eyes I had seen tonight, not to mention those I probably missed. "But you don't know who these drivers are. I'll take you home."

"YOU!" exclaimed Ava and Gina in unison.

"Yes, me! Why not me? I can drive, ladies. I do have my driver's license."

"I wasn't suggesting you couldn't but this is your party, your family party. You can't just leave."

"Why not? Yes, it is my family party, which is precisely why I need to make sure you, my assistant, gets home safely. Unless you want Luke to drive you?" I suggested it, knowing fully well that she did not want Luke to drive her home.

"No, no, Luke, you stay here with Gina and enjoy yourselves." She turned her body to look me square in the eye. "You can't drive me. If I am in no state to drive myself, why would you be?"

"Because I've been drinking sparkling water since we left the study. Besides, I am the owner and CEO of a liquor company, I can hold my own." Ava shook her head in agreement.

"You really want to drive me home?" she asked with curious eyes.

"Yes. Yes, I do. Come on, let's go."

"Ok, if you insist." She turned to Gina, patted her bulging abdomen and gave her a kiss on the cheek. "I'll see you Monday? Enjoy yourself. Have fun while you can!"

"Thank you, have a good rest of the weekend. Call me tomorrow, don't forget!"

"Ok, ok, I will." She turned to Luke. "Bye Luke, thank you for everything tonight. Have a good night." They gave each other cheek kisses and Luke shook my hand.

"You," said Gina, waving her finger at me, "drive safe and no funny business."

"Gina, she is my assistant. Relax." I turned my attention back to Ava, "Shall we? After you."

We headed back into the party, past the dance floor, which was now crowded. Ava continued walking, never glancing back. She hedge the dance floor and walked along the wall past the high-top tables and the makeshift lounge area. I distanced myself to give her space. Just enough space to let it be known that she was with me.

I don't know if it was the influence of the alcohol or her rush to leave but as we walked past the lounge area, Ava neither acknowledged nor noticed Liam who sat on a plush white loveseat, taking a smoke. Liam, however, noticed her and he noticed me right behind her. I tipped my head in his direction and smirked his way as I walked past. Let him think what he wants to think.

His eyes traveled from Ava to me and back. The tick of his jaw didn't go unnoticed. It appeared I had found a weakness. That was when it occurred to me, as I saw the look in his eyes, a look all too familiar to me. He wanted Ava and that was when I knew without a doubt that his engagement to Samantha was a farce. Being affiliated with Ava may be exactly what I needed. Ava stopped and turned my way.

"Are we good to go?" She asked.

"Yes, let's get out of here."

We continued out the front door and I led her to my car. She was walking closer now, humming a song I didn't recognize. Maybe something new or maybe she was just tone deaf. Regardless, I found it cute. She hummed and hummed periodically, leaning on me for support. She held onto my arm as we walked down the hill to the lot of cars.

"Why is your car down here?" She asked.

"This is the parking lot," I stated matter-of-factly. "All the cars are here."

"Not the family cars. I saw Liam's car up by the entrance."

"Liam is the favorite," I said with a smirk.

"Really? Hmmm, I find that hard to believe."

"Not that hard to believe."

"You are the new CEO after all."

She kept humming as we walked. A light breeze picked up, blowing her hair over her shoulder, sending adrift the familiar scent of orange blossoms that I was well acquainted with. To my surprise, I felt her small hand find its way into mine and it hugged my hand with a faint grip.

She was holding my hand. Three hours ago, she hated me and now here she was holding my hand. I didn't mind and I didn't object. I couldn't remember the last time I held a hand but I do remember the last time I held her hand and that might very well have been the last hand I held. It felt small and soft wrapped in mine and I liked it.

"So?" She questioned, waiting for my response to a topic I didn't want to talk about.

"So what?" I asked, playing unaware.

"Why do you say Liam is the favorite if you were the one promoted to CEO?"

"I was named CEO because I'm the oldest, have the most experience and the most education." She was staring up at me, I could feel her eyes like laser beams but I kept looking ahead, leading us to my car. I didn't want to talk about Liam or the promotion or anything having to do with my family or Closter Enterprises. It was a wild night, that turned out pleasant and I wanted to enjoy this brief walk in peace.

"Here we are." I unlocked the car, my new car, my first purchase after stepping foot back in Vilamor.

"This is yours? This is nice!" She ran her hand over the shiny black body of my SUV. "I didn't take you for the type to have a family car."

I laughed out loud. "I've never heard anyone suggest a Porsche is a family car."

"Well, it is large, very spacious, you could most definitely fit two car seats in here without issue."

"Car seats, Ms. Agostini?"

"Yes, children's car seats or boosters, you know where kids sit."

"Yes Ms. Agostini, I know what car seats are but that was not part of the criteria when I purchased the car."

She shrugged and resumed humming. I leaned over and opened the car door to let her in. She stepped her strappy gold heeled foot up into the passenger side and soon after, we both paused at the distinct sound of fabric tearing.

Her eyes widened as she bit her bottom lip, her hand simultaneously grabbed at the fabric on her upper right thigh. My eyes darted to her exposed flesh. The dress already left little to the imagination but now I had full view of her upper thigh just below her hip bone and it was still a great looking thigh, even after 22 years.

"Oh shoot!" She cried. She adjusted her posture in an attempt to cover her thigh, but the dress was done. "Well, there goes this dress, guess it has made its final appearance. It's not mine, it's Gina's and now I've torn it."

"I don't think she'll be needing it anytime soon and we can have it fixed." I took off my tux jacket and used it to cover her lap. My thumb grazed her warm skin and her eyes fluttered to mine. "Here, my jacket, for propriety's sake."

"Thank you," she whispered, adjusting the jacket over her lap.

I walked around to the driver's side allowing the visual of Ava's thigh to remain in the forefront of my mind for only those few moments before getting in and starting the engine. "I'll cover the cost to fix the dress," I assured her.

"No, no, you don't have to do that." She shook her head.

"You tore it getting into my car. Just take it to my dry cleaner next time you pick up my suits and have them put it on my tab. At the rate we are going, I'll need to buy a dry-cleaning service. Coffee spills and now we are tearing dresses." She laughed and I smiled as I backed out of the spot. I liked making her laugh, it was a sound I could never tire of hearing.

She leaned her head back on the headrest. I could feel her soft gaze on me.

"Are you going to tell me what you are thinking about?" I asked.

"Just thinking what a nice night I ended up having. I was dreading tonight. I didn't really want to come."

"Why is that?"

"The truth?" she asked with a sigh. I nodded. "I hated you."

"Hated?" I looked her way to see her nod while biting on her bottom lip. "That's a strong word."

"You haven't exactly been easy on me or polite for that matter."

"Ok, I can agree." I turned my attention to her as we approached a red light. "You said hated? Past tense. You don't hate me anymore?"

"Um, I didn't say that I don't." She twisted in her seat, making my tux jacket slip to the floor and I couldn't help but let my eyes wander the length of her creamy thigh. The same thigh that hugged my hips as we rode on my Vespa all those years ago. How many times I had wanted to touch her thigh?

She spoke, bringing me back to the present day. "You may be redeeming yourself. You were different tonight."

"Maybe we just misread each other. We are both a little too proud to admit when we are wrong." She remained silent and still in her seat. "Am I really the only reason you didn't want to come tonight?"

"No. I was torn about Liam. I was anxious to see him. Very excited but I was worried."

"Why is that? You both apparently had a good work and non-work relationship, no?"

"Yes, we did. Strictly platonic, I promise you." Her eyes were wide, just as they were the day, I took her down from the cliff and I knew she was telling the truth. "It's just. I don't know if I should tell you this. I'm clearly talking too much. Must be the scotch you gave me."

I laughed at her honesty. "Tell me."

"Liam and I, we always had a really good relationship. Very open or at least I thought we were open. We'd talk after hours. He met my kids. Then the day he left, he gave me no explanation and before leaving, he kissed me. A real kiss, on the mouth. It opened a door of possibilities you know, delusional possibilities but still a girl can dream."

She smiled and rolled her eyes. "I was excited to see what would happen when he returned, then he is gone for a month, I don't hear from him and he returns engaged. I don't know, I'm just confused. Just a reminder about trust."

Trust? Had I just stumbled upon one very important personality trait? One that seemed so foreign and different from Frankie.

"You trusted Liam?"

"I did, I think I did. It was the closest I have gotten to allow myself to trust a man in years. But my intuition was correct."

"Your intuition?"

"Yep! A man can't be trusted."

I processed her words. Such a jaded view to have, especially for someone who was so carefree and positive in her youth. It occurred to me that I was also not trusted and how much I would like to make her trust me. We remained quiet for the rest of the ride.

Her words played over and over in my mind. Hearing of her closeness to Liam and the relationship she had hoped for with him had my wheels turning. We approached her road and I knew I was running out of time. I spoke without hesitation, "Ava, I have a business proposition for you. Can you meet me Monday morning?"

"Business proposition? Can we discuss it in the office?"

"I'd rather discuss it outside the office. Can you meet me at 9:00 at Café Avignon?"

"Hmmm, I don't like how this sounds."

"I think you will be interested in this proposition."

"Well, I'd be a few minutes past 9:00, I have to drop the kids off."

"That's fine. Come when you can."

We arrived at her home. It was a quaint, tidy home. Perfect for two little kids to grow up in.

"We have arrived," she said as she turned to me. "Thank you for the ride home. I really didn't want to take Luke away from Gina. They need a night together to enjoy themselves before the baby comes. They are both so great together, aren't they?"

I nodded, agreeing. "They are. They are perfect for one another and they know it too. They have a good thing."

"They do. That's what I want," she said with a sigh, resting her head back on the seat and closing her eyes.

"Sorry to break it to you, Ms. Agostini but you are married, with children."

"I know," she smiled. "I meant I want that, what they feel for each other. I want to be with someone who thinks I am perfect."

I don't know why but her words hurt, they tugged at my chest. Hearing her confess that perhaps she wasn't perfect for her husband filled me with a great sadness that I couldn't understand.

"Closter, thank you for being the distraction and confidence I needed to turn tonight around. I had a great time." She leaned forward toward me, her hair falling over her shoulder. She lingered for a while and then brought her face closer to mine, placing a kiss on my cheek. "Have a good night," she said on an exhale.

"Good night, Ms. Agostini and the pleasure has been all mine."

Chapter 17
Nicholas

I spent the remainder of the weekend reliving the events of the party and my time with Ava. I mulled over the various possibilities and the probability of Liam being the cause of the sudden disinterest in the Laurent's willingness for acquisition.

Closter Enterprises was so engrained in who I was that it was difficult to fathom that my brother didn't equally wish for the perpetual success of the business. I was having second thoughts about my plan. It was nervy and completely unbrotherly.

But then it sank in that my brother was engaged to my ex. That alone made me bitter. It didn't take much further persuasion to decide that my plan would need to move forward. I pulled up to the parking lot in front of Cafe Avignon. I purposely picked that location.

It was private enough for conversation, close to her kids' school and at this point, it was fast becoming 'our spot', as all significant exchanges between us occurred in that very plaza.

I stepped out of my car on another beautiful day and looked up at the clear sky, thankful again to be back in Vilamor. I locked my Porsche, the very same car Ava sat in less than 48 hours ago. In fact, it still vaguely held her scent.

I strolled toward the café, walking past the sidewalk grate where Ava's heel had gotten wedged. I smiled to myself at the memory. With each passing day, I became more convinced that everything in life happens for a reason, even one's heel getting caught in a grate.

I took a table outside; the same table we had sat at just days before. I laid the napkin across my right leg, pulling my cell phone out of my pocket as a young girl, maybe college age, appeared before me.

"Bonjour, Mr. Closter!" She was overly enthusiastic for this hour of the morning. Clearly, she knew who I was and she didn't try to hide her excitement.

"Bonjour." The owners of Cafe Avignon were true Frenchmen, they had come over from France and this café was their life. I had gotten to know the owners. They were very proud of their heritage and had poured everything they had into the café, making it as authentic and French as possible from the coffee they brewed down to the pastries they baked. Having lived in Paris for over a decade, I could vouch for the quality.

"What can I get you this morning, sir?"

"I'll have an espresso. I'm also having a guest join me and I understand she enjoys your croissants, so please bring me a few chocolate and butter croissants with an assortment of jams. She'll have a cappuccino too. Thank you."

"Very well, sir."

The girl trotted back inside leaving me alone amongst the empty tables that occupied the outdoor cobblestone eating area. It gave me a rare opportunity to sit alone with nothing to do but observe those that walked past in the morning bustle to get wherever they needed to get to.

I looked at my phone through the sun glare. 9:03 a.m. She should be arriving soon.

And then I felt her.

I sensed her presence before I even saw her. The air changed when Ava was around. It became lighter. The air became thinner and vibrationally charged. There was an electricity, a pull I couldn't explain. I smelled her fragrance as I turned to see her approaching the table, her figure wrapped in sunshine.

She looked simple, classic, tranquil. Wearing a high ponytail, white sleeveless blouse, black skirt and perfectly toned legs that wore the same black high heels that got caught in the grate. She walked with a bounce, a natural bounce and she smiled as she pulled back her sunglasses.

"Good morning!" She said cheerfully.

The waitress approached, putting down the plates holding her croissants and small pots of jam. "I'll be right back with your coffees."

"Thank you," I said, standing to greet Ava with a kiss to her cheek. "Good morning," I replied, inhaling her sweet fruity scent.

She looked up at me stunned, "Are we on kissing terms now, Mr. Closter?" She smiled jokingly.

"You certainly thought so Saturday night." She blushed at my response. "Perhaps outside of work, why not? I think we are past formalities," I suggested.

"Ok, ok. I'll let that pass." She took the seat across from me, putting her handbag in the chair next to her, just as she had Friday afternoon. How different these two days felt.

"You look happy and chipper this morning."

She snickered. "You wouldn't have said that if you saw me yesterday. I was not feeling the best."

"Oh, why is that?"

She rolled her eyes. "Oh, I don't know. Guess you can blame the liquor you kept giving me." She laughed.

"Oh, is that so? Mama Bear had a hangover?" I asked. "Can't handle your liquor?" She nodded in response. "You can admit you had fun while you drank."

"Yes but I can't be doing that very often." She looked at the table, watching as the waitress placed her cappuccino and my espresso beside the arrangement of croissants.

"Thank you." She said in delight.

She scanned the spread laid out before her and her face brightened. "You ordered me croissants!" She said enthusiastically, "and a cappuccino!"

"Yes. You said they were the best here. Your favorite. I wasn't sure if you wanted the chocolate or the plain, so I ordered both."

"Thank you, Mr. Closter and for the record, chocolate, always chocolate. Chocolate everything!"

She looked happy today and I liked that she was happy. I liked that I could do something to make her happy.

"So, what's up?" she asked with a sigh, "Why did you invite me here?" Always to the point.

"Like I said, I have a business proposition. Let me preface this by saying everything I discuss with you today at this table is confidential. I know as my assistant I don't need to worry about discretion?"

"Obviously!" She fidgeted with her napkin before placing it across her lap. "I do want to put it out there that I already don't like the sound of this." She looked uneasy; I could tell from how she bit her lower lip. "Well, what is it? Out with it. What are the details?"

"I'll keep it brief, as the details aren't important." I adjusted the napkin on my lap, exhaling as I prepared to talk. "Laurent is pulling out of the deal. Not that they have told me but I heard it through my industry connections."

"What? You are kidding! All lights were green as of last week!"

"Yes, I know. Very sudden but then again, so is my brother's engagement. Don't you think?" I paused to take in Ava's reaction. "I believe that their engagement has nothing to do with love and everything to do with money, greed and power."

"Huh? I'm not following."

"Laurent, my brother is engaged to Samantha Laurent."

"Oh, my goodness," her eyes went wide, "I didn't realize they were tied."

"Yes, Samantha is Monsieur Jacques Laurent's granddaughter. No reason to get into the family drama or long-drawn-out history but my brother isn't exactly on board with my promotion. He expected it for himself. He is also being relocated to the Paris office. Long story short, he's jeopardizing my latest acquisition in the same manner a spoiled toddler would throw a tantrum."

"Doesn't this seem a little farfetched? Wouldn't he benefit from the acquisition too? He is a Closter, after all."

"My brother only looks out for himself; he doesn't see the big picture. I'm not sure what his plan is but it seems rather interesting timing that he is engaged to Samantha the same week issues have arisen with the acquisition."

"What makes you so sure he hasn't fallen head over heels in love with Samantha? And her with him?"

This was the part I hated having to verbalize. "Because I dated Samantha for four years and we went our separate ways Valentine's Day. Only after she pushed me for an engagement and I told her I had no intentions of getting married."

Ava's eyes grew wide. "Wow! Your brother is engaged to your ex?" I nodded. "So, the engagement is fake?" She asked.

"I don't know that answer, not yet anyway. Regardless, it's kind of shitty for a brother, don't you think? Either he is doing it for purposes of fucking me in business or he's an asshat who's screwing my ex."

Ava nodded, agreeing. "I'm sorry."

"Listen, I can't say I am surprised. He is spoiled, always has been and I know he isn't happy about not being promoted. I just can't believe that it is reason enough to interfere with the business."

"So, what do you need me for?" she asked between sips of her cappuccino. And now came the fun part.

"It occurred to me Saturday night that my brother wants you. He likes you. He may even love you but at the very least, he lusts for you. I saw it in the vehemence in his eyes toward me when he saw me leaving with you." Ava shifted uncomfortably in her seat.

"I need to keep that going. I need to get him to the point of not wanting to see you with me. To get him to the point of admitting he wants you. Maybe then he or Samantha, one of them at the very least, would come to their senses."

"I'm just having a hard time believing any of this. You brother is a good guy or at least that is what I thought."

"Good people do bad things sometimes. I'm not saying he isn't into Samantha or saying that he is. He is betraying me either way. Can you blame me for wanting to end it?"

"True but you are saying you think the engagement is a farce?"

"No one had any idea they were even dating or seeing each other prior to a month ago. You said yourself he never spoke of her."

"Yes but true love can make you do strange things."

"Perhaps. I wouldn't know," I said flatly.

"So, it was a quick engagement?" She asked.

"I was dating her nine months ago. We dated for four years. She gave me a choice, propose or she'd walk. I didn't propose."

"So, you are banking on either Liam or Samantha coming to their senses and breaking off the engagement."

"Yes. Both have ulterior motives."

"What do you want from me?" Straight to business, she was. Ava was going to be a hard one to crack.

"Just attend a few functions with me, as if we are dating."

"Make them jealous?" She asked.

"Precisely."

"And how do we end it? There's an expiration to this, right? When and how do we cut it?"

"We aren't labeling it. We are just going to be attending functions together. Hang out together a few times. You know, let people think what they want. Hopefully, this works sooner than later. If my gut is correct, then Liam or Samantha will end things before they walk down the aisle. Either way, we cut it once the Laurent deal is done. If they are stupid enough to get married, it's on them."

Ava shook her head in agreement. "As far as you and I go, you are worried about your reputation, so I'll take all the responsibility. I'll get on a girl, flirt, whatever—"

"Gotcha, move on and we will come to terms with the fact that you cannot settle down. We end it cordially and friendly. Preserving your playboy image at the same time."

"Yes, basically." I scratched my chin, absorbing her words. "My playboy image?" I asked, confused. "Am I a playboy?"

"Well, you are in your 40s and never married."

"Does that make me a playboy?" I questioned. I suppose I was but she didn't need to know that. Relationships took too much effort. Effort that I would rather use in business where I knew I would be successful.

"I don't know. Why would a good looking, wealthy man like yourself be unmarried? No wife or family of your own. It certainly paints the picture of being a playboy. Not to mention the list of females that have been attached to your name."

"List of females, huh? You've been following me?"

"No, I didn't say that. I might have typed your name into a search engine." She smirked.

"Maybe I just haven't met the one." I gazed intently at her, purposely making her uncomfortable and I liked it.

"Why me? You could do this with anyone. I am sure you have a little black book full of willing and able options. Every entry in that book of yours is probably more than willing to cooperate with your little plan and give you sex too. So why me?"

"You have a vested interest in this. And you're the one Liam wants. It would only work with you. Liam wants you; Samantha wants me. I want Laurent to close the deal. This will benefit us both. I also don't need to promise you anything or try to convince you that this is anything more than a charade."

"Anyone else would try to make it into a relationship. Their goal throughout would be to get me into a relationship. With you, I know you aren't interested." Ava shook her head, agreeing.

I cleared my throat. "I also like you more than is usual for me." Her head tilted to the side as she absorbed my words.

"I find that hard to believe. You have been nothing but rude to me most of the time."

"I think we have both been off-putting. It is nothing that can't be fixed. Besides, I think this will be fun with you." I continued, "You will make it pleasurable."

She continued enjoying her breakfast, watching me, listening with an unaffected appearance. Perhaps she did not want to do this. It would be wrong for me to force her and I didn't want her to think it was required or part of her job. "If, however you feel you can't do this or are in jeopardy of forming an attachment, let me know and I will seek a different plan."

She detached from our conversation, moved her gaze to the croissant on her plate and picked up the butter knife, dipping it into the strawberry preserve. I sought an answer in her face, in her demeanor but I couldn't read her.

"I'm not the relationship type Ms. Agostini, so please remove any bud of hope that we can form a relationship. I'm not interested, I don't do relationships, don't do marriage and don't do kids."

She put the butter knife down calmly and adjusted her posture. "What makes you think I am interested in a relationship or marriage? Least of all with you?"

"I can be quite charming. So, I've been told. Few resist me," I said jokingly.

Her eyebrow shot up. "Closter, you have been an asshole to me basically since the first time I stepped into your office." She sat back in her chair and folded her arms. "Let me put your fears to rest. Firstly, you are not my type. Secondly, I am not your type. Thirdly, I am already married. And finally." She looked away and ceased the conversation.

"And finally," I urged on.

"And if you must know, my opinion on marriage." She paused again. "Marrying someone is the most vulnerable and scariest of decisions that can be made and I don't want to ever be put in that situation again. I don't intend to marry again. So, you don't have to worry about me seeking any attachments."

"Someone who did it once and isn't interested in doing it again. I can respect that," I said. "I think we have an agreement; I'll have the contract drafted."

"Contract?"

"In my position, being your boss, I would like to have something in writing, should you choose to file a harassment complaint. Feel free to add your own clauses. I'll also add the pay."

"The pay?"

"This will take more of your time than what you spend at the office."

"No. No pay. That will just make me feel dirty. I am doing this for a good reason, I don't want to be compensated."

"Ok, as you wish. Of course, if you want sex, that I can do, just not a relationship." I knew I'd get a rise out of her with those words and it delighted me to see that they did.

Chapter 18
Ava

I was enjoying myself. I rarely got to sit down for breakfast. I was usually stuffing a roll in my mouth and sipping a cold coffee while I dropped the kids off at school. Sitting at this little table, enjoying the sunshine, a large cappuccino and a warm breakfast was a rare treat. The croissants were to die for and I thought it was so sweet that Nick remembered that I like them.

I know this meeting was for business purposes but I couldn't help but feel like it was also a truce, a real truce. We had turned a page Saturday and he no longer saw me as an adversary. And then just when I was having better feelings about him, he said the three-letter word and I just about spit up my coffee. Just when I thought I could do this.

"Sex? You are talking about sex!" I exclaimed. The gall of this man pushing the envelope.

"Yes, why not?" He asked, the corners of his lips lifting into a smirk.

"Because we won't be having any, that's why. So why bother bringing up the subject?"

"None? Not even to try?" He responded.

"Try sex? Who goes around trying sex?" I chuckled. "No, this isn't a test drive at a dealership. I'm not a pair of shoes to 'try' out."

Nick took a sip of his espresso and quickly placed the little cup back on the saucer with a loud clumsy thud. "Fuck, that's hot!" His reaction and words took me back to the day we collided outside the café. He dried off his lips, tapping them with the corner of his napkin.

"Now listen here Ava, I have never been monogamous, never faithful and that's even when I had the opportunity to be faithful and monogamous with a very willing and desirable partner. So how I am now expected to go without any?"

The audacity of this man! Seriously? Did he really for one second think this little deal of his would come packaged with intimacy! "Let me remind you, Closter that this fiasco is your brainchild, not mine, and I have no issues ending it seeing as it hasn't even begun!" It rushed out of my mouth with no thought in place like a running sentence that left me out of breath. "I will not have sex with you and we will not discuss that topic anymore."

Nick was now very much staring at me, studying my features and I could see the wheels of his mind turning as he formulated his next statement. "Why not? Do you not find me attractive? I'm very good in bed."

"Ha!" I almost choked on my cappuccino. Nicholas Closter certainly was not Liam Closter. Liam never would have spoken about sleeping with me. Nick's moral and social compasses were all off kilter. He was my boss! This could not be more inappropriate. This man before me was not the 19-year-old boy I had met years ago.

"Well now, what is so funny?" He questioned.

"The fact that you think yourself good in bed. Everyone thinks they are good in bed," I added.

Nick adjusted his posture. "I've never left anyone unsatisfied, believe me."

"Ok, whatever Closter," I said, annoyed. This was a mistake. I could sense it now. Big mistake. Was it too late to back out?

"So, answer my question."

"What question?" I barked.

He leaned in close, the smell of his aftershave dancing around me. I could feel his eyes searching for mine but I did not look up. "Do you find me attractive?"

I was now officially and admittedly uncomfortable. I adjusted in my chair, avoiding eye contact. I needed a distraction. I desperately needed to get this meeting over with. Food always distracted me. I grabbed Nick's biscotti from his saucer. He didn't seem to care or even notice.

He was too busy staring me down, waiting for my answer. I swirled the biscotti in my cappuccino, the foam and cinnamon mixing about. I so hoped he would get tired of waiting and move on, only he didn't. He kept staring at me, waiting and I was getting hot from his stare. I finished chewing before finally looking up.

"Well?" He questioned.

"Yes Closter, yes, you are attractive. But don't flatter yourself, it doesn't mean I want to have sex with you."

The answer he wanted. He let it be known by giving me his beautiful Closter smile. Liam had the same smile. I answered his question but he did not move on. It just opened the door to more questions. "When's the last time you had sex? You said you were never intimate with my brother. Were you dating while you were investing your time in him?"

"That's none of your business. Why are you asking me these questions?"

He nodded his head. "Ok, that is a yes, you did. Also, I am asking you these questions merely to get to know you. We do need to get to know each other if this is going to work."

"No!" I exclaimed, "No, I was not having sex. I did not have sex. When would I have time? Do you forget I am a single working mom?"

"There is always time for sex." He smiled devilishly. Why was he still staring at me?

"No, ok, there was no partner during or after your brother."

Nick's eyes widened with interest. "Before then?"

"Before?" I asked. "As in before my platonic relationship with your brother?" Nick nodded. "Well, yes of course. I was married, Closter!" I said with a huff, folding my arms over my chest, outraged at the topic of conversation and how it had gone in this direction so quickly.

Nick straightened his posture, sitting back in his chair. He adjusted his suit jacket. "I'll be damned!" He said. "Are you telling me that you haven't had any relations since your husband?"

I laughed, "We are all proper now using the word relations." I chuckled. Nick made a hand motion as if directing me to go on. "Yes, Closter, you are correct."

"I don't believe it."

"Why not?"

"He's been gone for years, Ava."

"Yes, I am well aware that my husband has been gone for years!"

"Ok. Ok, well why the hell not?"

"It's none of your business!" I whispered in outrage.

"Well, you can't tell me that there haven't been suitors, as I know you'd have no issue getting someone more than willing to do the act."

"I don't like it," I blurted out before I even realized I said it and I wished I could take it back.

Nick's interest was really piqued now.

"I'm sorry, did I just hear you say you do not like it?" He waited for a response and received none. "You do not like sex?" He asked again.

"Yes, yes, correct Closter. I do not like sex. Can we now move on from this topic?"

"Yes, I can tell you are uncomfortable. We can move on but you, my dear, have been deprived." Nick smiled suddenly, very much interested in this topic and wanting to further it but knowing when it was time to step away and let the course of time take over.

"Take that smile off your face, Closter. It ain't happening between us and as far as you are concerned, you can have sex," I said. "With other women. As often as you want. I don't care. This isn't a real relationship and I could hardly care who you take to bed."

Nick's eyes sparkled and he didn't budge, making me all that more uncomfortable.

"Ok," I said, putting my stuff together and throwing my sunglasses back on my face. "I have to go. I'm going to be late and don't want to anger my boss. He's a stickler for being on time and he already thinks I get beneficial treatment," I said, sticking out my tongue in jest.

***

Nicholas

I grinned as she stood to leave. I welcomed her joking gestures. A week ago, she would not have teased and been so playful. I understood that she was embarrassed by the conversation but as she left without any additional words, I couldn't help but feel sad to see her leave. I wanted more.

I watched her walk down the sidewalk toward her car. My eyes didn't leave her until she pulled out of her parking spot. God, she made me feel 19 again and I had definitely acted 19 by the direction that conversation had gone. What the hell was I thinking? I couldn't explain my behavior. All I knew at this moment was that I hadn't felt this alive in years.

I glanced at Ava's cappuccino mug, the last remaining evidence of her. The clear mug was dusted with cinnamon and the remnants of frothy milk. The rim was lined with her glossy, pink lipstick. A perfect imprint of her bottom lip. .

I leaned closer to the table, staring at the lip mark; both fascinated and obsessed. I placed my hand on the mug, palming it like I would a woman's cheek and I rubbed my thumb along the lip stain. This was the closest I had gotten to touch her lips.

I brought my thumb to my mouth and sucked the sweetness. I tasted cinnamon, coffee and something uniquely Ava that reminded me of honey. It tasted like heaven or the closest I'd ever get to heaven.

How long had it been that I had wanted to taste those lips?

July 2000

She hugged me tightly while her body shook with nerves, as I placed her on firm ground.

"Thank you, thank you, thank you," her sweet, shaky voice repeated. Her arms hugged tightly around my neck and her head rested on my shoulder.

"You're welcome," I replied as she released my neck and planted her feet on terra firma. "I don't know if I want to know what you were doing on that cliff. I'll save that for another conversation. I'm just glad I got here when I did."

"That makes two of us," she confessed.

"You're a ball of nerves." My eyes roamed over her frame, making sure she wasn't hurt. She was pretty. She was young. How old was she? I couldn't

tell. She had a young face but her body was something else. She wore cut-off jean shorts and a white tank top that left little to the imagination.

"Would you like to come with me for a ride?" I asked, pointing to my Vespa. "Maybe it will help you relax and get over this." She looked back over her shoulder at my Vespa and then back to me. Her eyes wandered over me silently.

"Sure."

"Great. I should probably ask you your name?"

"Frankie," she answered.

I extended my hand out to shake hers. "Nice to meet you, Frankie. I'm Nick." I held her hand longer than I should. It became awkward until she giggled and I finally returned her hand.

I knew nothing about her except that I just helped her down from a cliff and that she was the most beautiful girl I had ever seen. I felt somehow connected to her now and forever. My eyes settled on her lips and I observed that hers settled on mine.

I felt an urge, an urge I had never felt. I wanted to kiss those lips, I wanted to discover them, discover her mouth and know how she tasted.

"How old are you, Frankie?"

"I am sixteen."

I did not peg her for sixteen years old. She was young still, too young for me to get involved with. I reeled in my emotions.

"Ok Frankie, let's go for a ride." One ride, it was one Vespa ride and then I would never see her again.

That's what I told myself.

A chair scrapped on the concrete at my side and the sound nudged me back to my current reality. I turned my head to find Luke standing behind me. He waved uncomfortably and took Ava's seat, zeroing in on the leftover food like a vulture. It didn't take him long to grab her uneaten croissant and claim it as his own.

I had brought Luke up to speed yesterday. He agreed that Liam's engagement was a ploy to jeopardize the Laurent deal. He also agreed that nothing would get under Liam's skin more than seeing Ava with me. My brother wanted to play dirty and I could play dirty too.

"She's gone already?" He asked. "That was a quick meeting."

"Yes."

"How'd it go? Looks like she took off in a hurry."

"She's fine. Everything is fine." I pulled out my wallet. "We are going ahead with the plan."

Luke took a second bite out of the croissant as he leaned back. Flaky dough crumbs landed on his lap as he brushed them off. "I suppose that is good. It is what you wanted, correct? And you? Are you fine? What's with that look on your face?"

"Just hungry," I sighed.

"Hungry? Why don't you order something?"

"Nah, not that kind of hungry, Luke. I just realize I've been famished and never knew it. Luckily, I just found the snack that will satisfy my craving." I stood and took out money from my wallet, dropping it on the table.

Luke was standing now too, with a discerning look on his face. He was quick to grab my arm, which he had never done. It took me by surprise. "Nick, don't. Please, I am asking you as a favor to me, please don't do anything to hurt her. Gina is super hormonal right now and she will kill me if you do anything to her cousin."

"Relax, I have no intentions of hurting her. I'm only curious what it would have been like if I hadn't been such a gentleman when I was 19." I glanced one last time at the mug she had been drinking from. I knew then that although this arrangement was for business, I was going to enjoy it and take whatever pleasure I could from it. I had a taste of Ava and I wanted more.

Chapter 19
Nicholas

I found myself more distracted at work than usual. The truth was it had become increasingly more difficult to be surrounded by Ava and my focus was slipping. This was unusual for me. I couldn't explain it. There was something hallucinogenic about her.

Her scent and her glossy lips were becoming a fast disruption to my workflow. I now knew how those lips tasted and I was ready for seconds. Just as disturbing or should I say irritating, was Luke at my ear every chance he got, asking me what my intentions were with Ava and begging me to not screw anything up before his baby brother's wedding.

I had almost forgotten about the upcoming nuptials. Luke's younger brother Christopher was getting married in a few weeks and this weekend was the engagement party.

"I know how you tend to get in your own head and all but for Chris, for my mom, please don't turn the wedding into a fiasco. No scenes," pled Luke.

"I'm not! Relax. Can we please stop talking about this? We have a conference call in 5 minutes and I'm done with this topic. We are at work now, Luke. Get your head back in the game," I said it, I preached it but my head certainly wasn't in the game this week.

"Yeah, yeah, sorry. I just feel really funny about all of this. Like mixing business with pleasure and its oil and water."

"What?" I questioned him, not following his convoluted explanation. "Luke, relax!"

We both walked into the conference room. It was a frustrating room that had a wall of windows, which was brutal for the Vilamor sun. The views were spectacular from this side of the building, although it wasn't like we could enjoy them as the blinds were drawn 90% of the time so that the sun glare didn't disrupt the view of the video conferencing.

In minimalistic style, it had a sleek 24-seat black table with white cushioned chairs. The walls were adorned with abstract black and white art that looked like pencil scribbling done by a three-year-old, which apparently people now called art.

The purpose of today's meeting was an update on current and potential acquisitions. Most of the staff were already seated, including Ava who sat at my right, ready to take notes. I took my own seat at the head of the table and Luke sat to my left.

"Good morning," I said as I took my seat. "Most everyone is here," I said, looking around, noticing only two vacant seats. Those of my brother and Gina, his now new assistant. "We'll give it two minutes and then start."

Ava leaned toward me and I wished she hadn't, as I now found her scent incredibly disturbing to not only my thoughts but also my bodily functions, which became easily side-tracked in her presence.

"Would you like a coffee?" She asked in a barely audible whisper. "Since we have a few minutes to spare?"

I felt my clarity slipping. "That would be great. Yes, please and thank you."

I didn't really want or need another coffee but it would buy me some distance and allow my body an opportunity to slow my racing heart. I watched her leave and moments later, Gina walked in. She was without Liam and took her seat at the opposite side of the table, giving a little coy wave to Luke.

"Good morning," she said to the room.

Everyone responded with similar greetings.

"Gina, where is my brother? We are all ready to start."

"Ah," she scratched her head, looking behind her and then turned her attention back my way. "He was right behind me but he returned to get a coffee." Gina's cheeks turned red and I knew she was lying.

"Maybe he is still on Parisian time," I said flatly. "Excuse me." I stood up to go look for him.

"I can get him," suggested Luke.

"No, I got this one." The little shit wasn't going to walk around the executive floor and disregard the company flow. This meeting had been on the calendar for weeks and per usual, this was a weekly meeting that was always held promptly at 11:00 am to review our standings with our acquisitions. That's how it had always been and how it would continue to be.

I rounded the corner in the direction of the break room. I was sure he took the opportunity of an empty executive floor to approach Ava. Everyone was in the conference room and oddly, he and Ava were not.

I didn't want to come across as an angered boss or worse yet as possessive or jealous. I counted backward from ten to distract myself and adjusted my tie as it felt as though it would suffocate me.

On the other side of the corner, I found both Liam and Ava in the hall just outside the break room. Ava held a cup and saucer with what I presumed was my coffee. She had even placed a small biscotti per usual on the side. Damn she was good at her job, going above and beyond.

She looked flustered, uncomfortable and her body was tilted not in Liam's direction but in the direction of the conference room, as though she had been walking back when Liam caught her attention. I cleared my throat as I approached. Both Liam and Ava followed the sound in my direction.

"Mr. Closter," Ava's eyes settled on me. "I was just returning with your coffee." She looked down at the cup and saucer.

"You are both late," I said flatly.

"I'm sorry. I was headed back when—"

"My fault, big brother," Liam said, cutting Ava off mid-sentence. He puffed out his chest, "I was just touching base with Ava about Chris and Alana's engagement party. We had made plans; I was going to pick her up but now—"

"But now you have another woman to worry about," I said, interrupting him. "I am sure Samantha wouldn't appreciate you taking another woman in her place."

"Right," he responded. "So, I just wanted to make sure Ava was all set with her plans and how she would get to the party."

"Yes." Ava, straightened her spine. "It is all fine, Liam. I do drive," she said with a forced smile. "I'll be there, wouldn't miss it."

"Yeah, of course. I just feel bad."

"Nothing for you to feel bad about, Liam. Ava and I are going together." We hadn't discussed Chris' party or the wedding but surely with our new agreement, I would take her. She wasn't going alone.

I watched them both, taking in their reactions. Ava clearly was surprised and Liam, although trying to appear cool, had the dead giveaway of flaring nostrils. He didn't like it. Good. Get used to it little brother, you're going to be seeing Ava and I together a lot more than just around the office.

"You are going together?" He asked, looking from me to Ava. Ava shook her head but gave no verbal response.

"Can we get back to work now?" I asked.

"Yes," answered Ava as she started back toward the conference room, her heels clicking on the marble floor. I turned to also return.

"What are you doing?" Liam asked in an angered tone.

"Going back to our meeting that was scheduled for 11:00 a.m. and it's now past 11:00."

"You know what I mean!" He said impassively. I struck a nerve. I knew it and I liked it. "With Ava."

"Ava is none of your concern. She never was but she certainly isn't now. Why don't you worry about yourself and your new fiancé, Samantha?"

"You touch one hair on her head and I'll destroy you."

"Careful with the threats, Liam. Does Samantha know you are so protective over Ava? Tell me little brother, how does it feel to be engaged to one woman but in love with another?"

"Shut up." He started walking back to the conference room, purposely knocking his shoulder into mine as he walked past.

It felt good to strike a nerve. Liam was always the golden child, always the preferred and always taking what should be mine. He took my seconds when he took Samantha, maybe he thought that would anger me. Maybe he did it to jeopardize the Laurent deal. Whatever his reason, I now knew with 100 percent certainty that he had feelings for Ava and now the ball was in my court.

I straightened and returned to the conference room behind him. He took his seat on the nearest end of the conference table near Gina and I went to the head of the table between Ava and Luke.

"Everything ok?" asked Luke, leaning in.

I gave him a short nod, returning my attention to the paperwork that lay in front of me. I concentrated on the agenda and tried to get back into the zone. The small white cup and saucer with my espresso caught my eye. Ava. Thank goodness for Ava knowing exactly what I needed before I knew myself. I brought my eyes up and stared my brother straight in the eye.

He was still on edge. I saw it in his appearance and I wanted to keep him there. I held my eyes on him as I neared Ava. I leaned close, closer than necessary but I wanted to aggravate Liam. He watched and his jealousy was visible by the flex of his jaw.

"Thank you for the coffee, Ms. Agostini."

She leaned further closing any remaining distance and whispered, "You're welcome. I got you a couple of biscotti as well. I noticed you didn't have any food with your morning coffee and thought you might be hungry."

I tried not to react but a smile took over. I nodded, completely satisfied at both my brother's glaring eyes and the fact that Ava thought enough about my wellbeing. I beamed at her as I covered her hand with mine and tapping it three times in a gesture of appreciation.

"Ok everyone, let's get to it. Good morning."

"Good morning," responded most everyone except my brother who looked as though he had better places to be.

We went through the agenda points, finally landing on the Laurent acquisition.

"Luke, is everything all set for the meeting in France with the Laurent's for the 22nd through the 24th?"

"Yes, you and I will fly out in the evening of the 21st and hit the ground running, reviewing inventory and current production stock with Jacques on the 22nd and then meet with the bank and the antiquities council on the 23rd."

"The antiquities council?" asked Liam. As Vice President of Marketing, Liam was the least physically involved at this point in negotiations and obviously he was rarely if ever interested in acquisitions, same as with anything else pertaining to work.

However, he was a Closter and did have ambitions for higher roles, so to say I was disappointed in the fact that he hadn't read the emails he was copied on was an understatement.

"Yes, as discussed in emails last week, the city council of Reims is not exactly supportive of a non-French organization associating as Champagne negociant. They want to meet and review their requirements to preserve the French image, etc." Explained Luke.

"I don't know if the purchase of the Laurent vineyards is in our best interest," added Liam. That statement was completely off topic and about six months too late. Everyone shuffled in their seats, facing Liam's direction.

"Why ever not? We have always discussed wanting to expand our line and sparkling wine seems the next most logical step."

"Perhaps I said it wrong. I don't think this acquisition is in the Laurent's best interest," clarified Liam and I was ready to blow a fuse.

"It was a month ago," I said, steadying my tone.

"Well, things change," he smirked.

"If by things, you mean your engagement to Samantha Laurent, let me remind you, you are a Closter first and foremost. You are Vice President of Marketing for Closter Enterprises. We purchase, manufacture, market and promote fine wines and liquors worldwide."

"Your job is not to review the interests of our acquisitions but rather to market and promote. If Samantha or her family are having doubts about the buyout, let me remind you that it is a very generous offer and your job is to make them see how generous an offer it is."

Liam shook his head in understanding. "Well, the 22nd through the 24th won't work. The Laurent's will be in Vilamor for my engagement."

"I spoke with Jacques myself on Friday and we were all set," stated Luke with a twinge of annoyance.

"Yes, well we decided yesterday that we will have our engagement party that weekend. The Laurent family will be coming to Vilamor that week to stay with us in preparation."

"Fine, we can discuss details. Luke, reschedule the visit to Reims. Meeting adjourned." I was fuming and didn't want to look at my brother a second longer than necessary. He knew what he was doing, provoking me with his attempted cool, calm attitude to undermine my months of work. The little shit was trying to make me look unprepared at my own meeting.

"I'll call Jacques right now," declared Luke, sounding equally as infuriated as me. "I don't understand, he seemed more than on board last week."

"I understand. His granddaughter is engaged to Liam and I am certain Liam has been in both Samantha and her father's ear about how they can grow the company on their own without the aid and need of a negociant."

Luke shook his head in disbelief. "I guess you were right all along."

"About what? My brother trying to take me down? I wasn't kidding, I just thought he cared enough about the company to not be so selfish as putting his spoiled desires ahead of all else."

"Let me talk to the old man and see where his head is at." Luke nodded in Ava's direction before filing out with the rest.

I was finally able to release the sigh I held for far too long. It was a sigh of frustration. I let my body relax against the chair. Ava's coffee teased at me again. How did she know I'd be needing it? It wasn't hot anymore but soothing all the same. I watched as Ava buzzed around, tidying up the conference room. It wasn't her job but I had seen her do it time after time after every meeting.

"You know we do pay for a cleaning crew."

"Yes, but they don't come until night-time and there are other meetings scheduled for today."

"It doesn't feel right having the executive assistant to the CEO clean up after everyone."

"Why not? Gina did it before me. I think it's always been the executive assistant's duty or expectation. Just as we are the ones to set up the room and order the refreshments."

I finished my coffee and gathered my papers to leave as Ava continued in prepping the room for the next conference.

"Besides, I like doing it. It is relaxing and gives me a mental break." A loud thud of something metal banged into a surface before falling to the ground. "Ouch!" cried Ava.

I looked up to see the projector screen had dislodged from the ceiling, hitting Ava on the head as it dangled from wires. She held her right hand to her forehead while steadying herself with her left hand.

I took quick strides toward her. "What the hell happened?" I surveyed her forehead. There was a nasty bump forming on her forehead but it also managed to catch her skin just right and she was bleeding. "You need to take a seat."

"The screen was jammed," she rambled to explain, "so I gave it a tug like we always do every time it is jammed but I guess maybe I tugged too hard."

"No. It shouldn't be getting jammed or loose enough for your simple tug to dislodge it. I'll have the tech group look at it. Come, take a seat." I picked her up by the waist, not thinking about my actions or how they would appear. I sat her down on top of the conference room table.

"I'm fine, Mr. Closter," she said, fixing her blouse and brushing me off.

"You're saying that because you haven't seen your forehead." I grabbed the phone from the center of the conference room table and dialed Gina's extension. "Hey, Gina, yeah, listen can you get me some first aid supplies? No, I'm fine, Ava just had a little accident in the conference room. Yes, thank you. Oh and please have IT come up here, let them know there is an issue with the projector screen. Thank you."

I placed the phone receiver back on the console and returned my attention to Ava. She had blood on her fingertips from where she tried to feel the injury and she was steadying her breathing.

"Here," I said, handing her my pocket square. "This is exactly why I don't want you doing these sorts of things."

"Mr. Closter—"

"Nick, call me Nick," I insisted.

"All the assistants do this. Just consider yourself lucky it was me; you won't need to worry that I will file a worker's comp claim," she joked.

"At least you still have your sense of humor."

Gina came rushing in. "What happened?" Her eyes went to Ava's forehead and she grew pale. "Oh my God Ava, you have blood." She turned a pale shade bordering on gray and squinted her eyes shut. "Oh my God, I'm sorry I can't stay to help, the sight of blood is literally making me sick. I'm sorry." She handed me the first aid kit and a box of tissues before quickly turning to leave. I grabbed a handful of tissues and blotted them against Ava's forehead.

"Is it that bad?" she asked, wide eyed.

"Here, why don't you see for yourself?" I lifted the bloodied tissues from her forehead to show her the evidence.

"Oh goodness. Well, gee, I guess I can't go to the party tomorrow," she sarcastically snapped her fingers with a grin as she stood from the table to leave.

"No, you don't!" I jested as my fingertips grazed her moving figure. I caught her from behind, grabbing at either side of her waist as I pulled her back to the conference room table. Her eyes scanned me as I lifted her back to the table where her legs now dangled between mine, caging her in so she wouldn't leave again.

"I'm fine," she protested, "I can do this myself."

"Listen, you got hurt in my conference room, in my office building while you were working for me. Let me do it. Ok? Just let me help." She rolled her eyes and exhaled, straightening her spine. I took that as a sign of acquiesce.

I opened the first aid kit, setting out the items I would need. "This might sting," I warned her.

"Thank you," she said meekly. I studied her face. Her porcelain face was petite but with mighty features that couldn't help but capture my attention. She kept her eyes locked on the floor, avoiding me and avoiding eye contact. I raised her chin, forcing her eyes to meet mine before I dabbed the alcohol-soaked cotton pad on her forehead. She flinched at the burn, closing her eyes as she rode out the pain.

"Sorry, sorry, just another dab then I'll put on the antibiotic lotion and bandage you up."

Her eyelashes fluttered like the wings of a butterfly as her lids lifted and her chocolate eyes fixated on mine. The air caught in my lungs as her breathing quickened, I could see it in the way her chest was rising and falling. My eye caught the pulse point of her neck, twitching rhythmically in time with her breathing.

It struck me then that she was nervous to be around me. Not at all the response I wanted to evoke in her. I brought my hand to her throat, laying my thumb over the center of her clavicle where her breathing was frantic and her pulse throbbed.

"Are you scared?" I asked as I watched her pounding pulse, fascinated, I rubbed my thumb back and forth over it. I searched her eyes for an answer but saw none. I tried to hide the thrill that I felt being this close to her but I failed miserably.

"Do I make you nervous?" I reworded my question. The tension built between us as I became overly aware of the feeling of her legs between mine. Ava didn't speak but her glare was unwavering. The heat radiating from her stare made me more confident to press on as I brushed my finger further past the warm pulse up her neck until I was cupping her cheek. She took a jagged inhale and held her breath. "Your pulse and your breathing betray you, Ava."

I leaned in, wanting to kiss her and so badly needing to taste her. Then something crossed over her eyes. I saw it briefly but I was experienced enough to know it was lust. Before I could act on it, it was gone as she shook her head.

"I feel better," she stated, clearing her throat. "And the bleeding has stopped."

"Knock, knock," interrupted Luke with a wavering voice, "sorry to intrude." We both moved to look at the door where Luke's presence loomed in the sunlight.

Ava jumped off the conference room table, her cheeks now pink with embarrassment. "I need to get back to work," she said self-consciously.

"I'll pick you up at 5:30 on Saturday," I said as I watched her head out.

"What?" She stopped, turning to me with furrowed brows.

"Chris and Alana's party—"

"Oh, right! You don't have to pick me up."

"Sure, I do. I want to. Besides, remember our deal?"

"No, please. I'd rather just meet you there. It'll be easier that way," she continued, hastening her steps toward the door. "Excuse me, Luke."

I watched her leave and returned to my seat, slumping in my chair. I needed to calm my racing heart before I gave myself a heart attack.

"We are fucked!" asserted Luke, shaking his head.

"Why? What happened?"

"You've got it bad for her."

"Is it that obvious?" I asked, dragging my hands down my face.

"Hell, yes!"

"I didn't touch her other than to clean her cut."

"You didn't have to touch her. You were basically straddling her, while you eye fucked her left, right, forward and back." Luke paced to the window. "Jesus, Nick! She basically ran out of here!"

"What's the big deal? You and Gina are married and both work here."

"I never came onto Gina at the workplace. Gina's also not my assistant."

"So, it is wrong for me but no one would think twice if it had been Liam and Ava."

"I'm just saying be careful, take it slow and stop looking at her like that."

"Like what?"

"Like you want to bend her over your desk."

I did want to bend her over my desk and so much more but Ava was different. I recognized that much and I knew I had to be different with her. I needed to soften my approach and take more friendly tactics rather than that of a predator. Honestly, I didn't want to be the predator and her, my prey. I acknowledged this change in me and it was frightening.

"It's difficult for me, Luke. I have this need to take care of her. I can't explain it. I guess it ties back to saving her on the cliff that first day." I got up and joined him by the window, looking out at the views. "I'll never hurt her or purposely try to make her uncomfortable."

"I know that, man but maybe try being friends with her first and not her boss. And definitely not some guy trying to come onto her."

Chapter 20
Ava

Finally, Friday night arrived! My favorite day of the week. I was filled with an all-consuming anxiety. I couldn't shake it. Something felt off. I felt it throughout dinner, while giving the kids their bath and now as I tucked them in for the night.

If I had to be honest, I was dreading the engagement party tomorrow. I went from never going out to suddenly my social calendar was taking over my home life. I had always been a homebody. As fun as getting dressed up and going out could be, it was all just starting to feel like a chore.

Furthermore, I didn't like how close Nick and I were getting. It was too close for my comfort. He made me nervous, in a way I couldn't understand and I couldn't avoid the strange sensations I felt around him. What happened in the conference room was dangerously foreign for me and I felt uneasy about being around Nick again. Not because I was afraid of him, I knew him well enough to have no fear, but because I was afraid of myself around him.

I placed my attention on my most loved Friday night activity. There was nothing I liked more than plopping onto my couch with a tray of snacks, a warm cup of tea and a Christmas movie. It was my only solace.

Now with the kids in bed, fast asleep, the house took on the quiet, lonely appearance it did every night at bedtime. This was when I relaxed but also when the sadness settled in. These were the hours I questioned the direction of my life and how it had turned out the way it did.

No one prepared me for how lonely being a single mom would be. The days were hectic, wild, overwhelming and then the nights were just so still, desolate and quiet.

I went around the house tidying up the toys, the balls, the books, the blocks all in time before the movie started. I tiptoed downstairs, ready to get cozy with my favored blanket, following a warm bath. I was replacing the top on my storage ottoman when I was startled by alarming scratching noises sounding from my window.

I walked to the window, convinced it was the shrubs rubbing on the side of the house. The ungroomed shrubs always brushed against the window when it was windy; however, when I pulled open the blinds, I jumped ten feet as I looked out and caught sight of a large figure outside. It was too dark to make out any features but I was sure I saw a man.

Oh crap, oh crap! What do I do? My worst nightmare was coming to life. When you were a woman living alone, this exact scenario played in your head often, if not constantly. This was the worst nightmare. For years, I kept these fears at bay, not wanting them to take over and become a fear for the kids too.

I knew I should have thought of a plan if a situation like this occurred but I never had. I quickly ran through what to do. The questions and thoughts flashed through my mind. Are all the doors locked? Yes.

Windows closed? I think so but I did have them opened earlier to let the breeze in. Oh no! I realized my cell phone was resting on the console table by the front door but I needed to get to it and call someone. The police? Yes.

I didn't have any weapons or anything even resembling a weapon. I looked around, scanning the living room and my eyes settled on the lamp. It had considerable weight, iron base and it was big enough to make an impact. It would have to do. I ran over to the side table, quickly unplugging it and tiptoed to the front door to grab my phone.

When I reached the front door, I heard muffled knocking. Oh no! This is it; this is the moment! My heart was racing. I was sure I was paces away from a heart attack. My hand shook as I held my phone and dialed the police on speaker phone. At least they could hear what was happening and send help for the kids.

I held the lamp in my right hand and grabbed the doorknob with my shaky left hand. I took in an unsteady, deep breath as I swung open the door, ready to clobber the intruder over the head. A suffocating gasp clenched my chest as I looked upon my assailant.

"Hey!" exclaimed the intruder.

"CLOSTER! What are you doing here?" I closed my eyes, resting my hand over my rapidly beating heart, trying to calm myself. Before me stood Nicholas wearing athletic pants, a hooded sweatshirt and sneakers. I had never seen him this casually dressed. He was carrying a brown paper bag and holding a cardboard tray with two beverages. He sneered unknowingly.

"Do you greet all your visitors holding a lamp?"

"I thought you were an intruder!"

"And the lamp was going to save you?" he asked with a chuckle.

"What are you doing here?" I asked impatiently.

"Hello," he said with a fake pout, "first things first, you should never open the door without checking to see if you know who is on the others side. I could have been a robber or worse."

"Hello and I am well aware," I said flatly.

"Vilamor police department, how can I help you?" We both jumped at the voice that came from the phone.

"Oh dear!" I picked up the phone, taking it off speaker and bringing it up to my ear. "I'm so sorry. I thought there was an intruder at my house but it's just my boss. I apologize. Thank you. Ok, yes, bye-bye."

I replaced my phone on the table and turned my attention back to Nicholas, aiming to get him out of my house as quickly as possible. "Closter, what are you doing snooping around my house?"

"I wasn't snooping. These are heavy bags," he said, lifting two brown paper bags, "I didn't want to ring the doorbell and wake your kids."

"Ok, well I'm not sure what you are doing here. You scared the living hell out of me! So, I called the police."

"I see and your weapon of choice is a lamp?" He grinned.

"I didn't have anything else near. Besides, I can't really hurt anyone or kill anyone. I'm not wired that way. The lamp would just give me enough time to run and lock the door."

He looked at me with furrowed, concerned brows. "Don't ever repeat that you aren't wired to hurt anyone. That information you keep to yourself, Ava. Do you understand? You need to think about the safety of you and your kids. And maybe we need to get you a camera out here so you can see who is at your front door before you decide whether or not you want to open it."

"We aren't doing any of that," I said, waving my finger between us. "Ok? Anyway, whatever. What are you doing here?"

"Why are you so frigid?"

"Excuse me?" I asked, confused by his change of conversation.

"You are so cold, so uninviting. I just want to be friends," he explained.

"I have friends," I stated point-blank.

"Can't you use another?"

"No. I keep my circle of friends small and tight."

"Frankie wouldn't object to making new friends."

"Frankie was sixteen and inexperienced."

"That is sad," he remarked with a melancholic look on his face. "When did you become so jaded?"

Was I? Had I become jaded? I couldn't answer that question. I was unsure myself.

"What are you doing here, Closter?" I asked, frustrated.

"I want to check on your head and make sure you don't have a concussion."

"I'm fine. Thank you."

"Ok, so we can watch the movie."

"What movie?" I was puzzled.

"The Friday night Christmas movie."

"You know about the Friday night Christmas movies? You watch Christmas movies?"

"I didn't know about them and I've never watched one but Gina said that is what you do every Friday and that they start at 8:00 pm."

"Gina?" I shook my head. "Of course. Why were you and Gina talking about my love of Christmas movies or my Friday night plans?"

"I know a date would be out of the question since you have the kids. Not to mention I don't think you have entirely warmed up to me. I figure I'd bring the date to you. I would have been here sooner but there was a wait at the sushi place."

"You got sushi?" I asked, intrigued. My interest was piquing.

"Yes, sure did. Sushi, chocolate croissants and two hot chocolates with mini marshmallows."

I shook my head, biting my lip, hoping to hold in my smile. "Those are some of my favorite things."

"Yes, I know," he said matter-of-factly with a wink. "Just some snacks and treats while we watch the movie."

"You want to watch the movie? With me? Seriously?"

"Yes, I want to see what all the fuss is about with these movies that consume your Friday nights." He walked into my house, slipping off his shoes, while still holding the bags and drinks. He looked around my home. "This is nice! It's cozy. Cleaner than I thought it would be."

"Excuse me?"

"With two kids, I thought there would be toys all around."

"Oh, well you came at the right time. If you had arrived half an hour ago, it would have looked like a war zone but the kids are now asleep and I have since cleaned up."

He seemed to study my response, taking his time to digest my words. "Hmm, I see."

"Yeah, that's my life, Closter. Messy house and messy life! It's loud, disorganized, there is yelling and tantrums and everything else that is unpleasant. You just caught me at the right time."

He nodded, not paying much attention to my words. "Through here, I see." He walked into the living room, depositing the drinks and bags on the coffee table. "Looks like the movie will be starting soon, you better get in here and get comfortable. I have all the utensils, plates and napkins that we will need right here."

I rubbed my temples. "You are really going to stay and watch this with me?"

"Yes."

"Uninvited?"

"Are you going to ask me to leave?" he asked with a grin.

"Uh, no, you are my boss. Not to mention you are Luke's cousin—"

"And we have a deal," he winked.

"Yes but the deal doesn't involve my free time."

"No, perhaps not but it will be easier to get to know each other outside the office and get more comfortable in each other's presence."

I stared at him, unsure what to say or how to react.

"Please?" He requested. I looked at the bags of food, the hot chocolates and the TV screen. It did all look and smell delicious. My eyes perused his comfortable attire and his calming aura. He had done all of this to spend time with me. I couldn't bring myself to turn him away.

"Ok," I conceded.

"Ok? Great!" He rubbed his hands together and waved me over.

"Now let me get a look at that bump," he said, moving closer. He rubbed his thumb over my head. "It is still pretty prominent but the cut doesn't look too bad anymore." He clapped his hands together. "Ok, have a seat and I'll get everything set up."

And that is how it went. He truly did think over every detail, nothing was missing and although he may not admit it, I think he actually ended up liking the movie. When it was over, I glanced at him and his face wore a smile.

"Can I ask, what do you find so appealing with these movies?" He asked.

"Oh, I don't know. I guess the way it all gets tied up in a pretty bow at the end."

"You like pretty bows?"

"Yes, I like pretty bows, Closter!" I laughed. "You know what I mean. It's romantic and the endings are sweet. They always end with a kiss and a promise of a happy future."

"Oh, I see. The fairy-tale!"

"I suppose? Perhaps because I didn't exactly get my fairy-tale or happy ending. There is always hope."

"There is always hope," he repeated. "I didn't take Ava or should I say Frankie as a hopeless romantic. Look at all I learned from one Christmas movie."

"Don't act so unaffected. I think everyone wants love and a happy ending."

"Possibly." We looked at each other with not much else to say and it became awkward. "I'm going to get going and let you catch up on your sleep. Tomorrow is a big night, Ava!"

"Oh goodness, don't remind me." I took a deep breath and clasped my hands around my waist. "Ugh, another party."

"Don't sound so excited! I've never heard of a woman who does not want to go out and get dressed up."

"I'm a homebody and I went from not going out, at all, to now all the sudden I have weeks of events to attend."

"It's only a few events and I promise to take it easy on you. I promise no more scotch for you." He tapped my nose with his index finger and I scrunched my face. He laughed as he gathered the trash to take with him. "I'll pick you up at 5:30."

"No, please. Remember, like I said before, I'd much rather meet you there. The kids will be here. It is just easier."

We both walked toward the front door. He hovered, seemingly trying to delay his exit. He looked at me as if he wanted to say something or do something but didn't. He just lingered by the door.

"Would you like to take the leftovers home?" I asked, not sure what to say or do to break the awkward silence.

"No, no, those are for you."

"Thank you."

"I'm going to go. I've occupied enough of your time. Good night, Ava."

"Good night, Closter. Drive safely."

I watched him stroll down my front steps toward his car. I felt jumbled. I closed my door abruptly, needing to distance myself. I was all too aware that I needed to see him again tomorrow and I didn't know how I would make it through another event while maintaining my strong independent façade. I was learning that it was a hard façade to preserve when in Nicholas Closter's company.

Chapter 21
Ava

Another night, another party.

"Ugh," I sighed, already physically and mentally exhausted. I hated parties.

I hurried about, multitasking. I juggled to get myself ready, get the kids fed and set them up for the night. The doorbell rang and I jumped out of my skin as I raced down the stairs, trying not to trip but wanting to get to the front door before the kids did. I was already running late and beyond frustrated with my uncooperative hair. The interruption with the door annoyed me.

I hurried to tie the satin belt of my pink robe before undoing the deadbolt. I swung open the front door and my stomach dropped. I was so flabbergasted, I was sure it showed on my face. There, on the other side of the door, stood Nicholas Closter.

Unlike the prior night, he presented today dressed in a full tux and looking too good to be in this neighborhood. Not that there was anything wrong with my neighborhood, it just wasn't the type of neighborhood that was frequented by ritzy, wealthy, tux wearing, handsome men. Without a doubt, my nosy neighbors were poking their heads out their windows and stretching their blinds to get a better view.

My heart pitter-pattered as I took in the yummy view of the devilishly handsome man that stood before me. Damn, why did he look so good! I was distracted and surely gawking. I blinked hastily, trying desperately to concentrate on what needed to get done.

"Closter!" I whispered through clenched teeth. "What are you doing here?"

"Hi, Ava." He breathed my name in a smooth mood. "You look fantastic!" He exclaimed in a new hushed tone. "Interesting choice of cocktail wear but then again, I find it hard to keep up with what you girls call fashion." His eyes appraised and paused at my chest where my hand clasped together the edges of the satin material. I fidgeted with it, aware of his stare, holding it just a little tighter.

"This is my robe!" I snapped. "I just finished my hair and make-up and was about to put on my dress before you interrupted me," I huffed, losing my patience with the conversation.

I glanced back up the stairs to see if the kids had heard the doorbell. Thankfully, they had not, as neither one of them had poked out their heads to snoop as usual.

"Closter, what are you doing here?" I asked again anxiously.

"Why are we whispering?" he asked with furrowed brows.

"Why are you here?" I asked.

"My father raised me that a gentleman should always pick up his date. It might be the only thing he taught me not related to the business world."

"Ok, well, we are whispering because my kids are upstairs and this isn't a date." I shook my head.

"Of course it is, Ava. It is a scheduled engagement that we are attending together. What else would you call it?"

I waved my hand to quiet him. Semantics were not important.

"I told you I would meet you there."

Nick disregarded my comments and barged his way past me into my home, again uninvited as he was yesterday.

"No, that won't do. If this is to appear legitimate, we must show up together. Everyone knows I like my arm candy and I show up with my arm candy. It is how I've always done it, Ava."

"Ok, whatever. Listen, I can't have you here. My kids are upstairs with the babysitter and they can't see you. What am I supposed to tell them if they see me leaving with you?"

"Just tell them we are friends."

I looked at my wristwatch. "Oh my God! Ok, ok, we can't have this argument because we are going to be late! Ok, come in, sit on the couch. That couch," I said, pointing. "And do not move! Do not make a sound."

I was frantic and maybe if he didn't make a sound, the kids would stay upstairs. "I need to go finish getting ready," I explained.

He walked further into the house and did a turn about my living room before taking a seat. I ran upstairs, praying Nicholas would follow my directions and not leave the living room. I equally hoped the kids would stay in their playroom. Answering to the inquisition that would come from my kids if they saw a man in the house was not part of what I wanted to do this evening.

***

Nicholas

I surprised Ava. I went against her request and I knew my presence in her home annoyed her. Yes, she did say she would meet me at the party but obviously, I couldn't let that happen. I had other plans for us. Besides, why have a date if not to show up with them?

I would do as she asked and stay in the living room quietly. However, patience was not a virtue of mine and I hated waiting. I never waited. I tapped my fingers on the edge of the couch, bored. I finally stood up, unable to sit any longer.

I strolled around the small room, looking at the pictures and trinkets she had sprinkled about. It was a cozy, homey living room that was tastefully done. Nothing loud, overstated or overly girly or obnoxious. It was a welcoming room done in peaceful hues of ivory and beige.

I felt right at home last night and hadn't bothered to look around. I had other things to grab my attention, namely Ava and her warm body that sat feet away from me. Tonight, I wanted to explore in more ways than one.

As I walked about, I saw not one picture of her husband. I expected I would. I didn't know what that schmuck looked like. I'd love to see that prick. My curiosity was taking over as I continued looking around. There were tons of pictures of the kids but no dad in sight. I wanted to see what type of man ended up winning over Ava's heart. What lucky bastard did she end up with?

The kids were cute and they were clearly all Ava. No one could mistake that smile or those eyes. Her genes were strong. Thank God, something in the universe was right as I could imagine it would hurt to look at your kids and see the face of the man who left you.

As I kept walking about, I concluded the photos were indeed just of the kids. All except one. Only one. It was a simple, candid black and white photo of a beaming Ava holding a newborn and a little girl in pigtails with the biggest smile on her face, sitting at Ava's side. It was a simple black and white photo but it radiated love and emotion.

I felt a tug in my heart and a tug at my pants. I looked down to see a small human.

"Hi!" Greeted the small voice of a little boy with short brown hair and large eyes that dominated his face. I remembered the face from that day at the preschool. This was Ava's boy. I felt my chest compress with an eerie feeling that had become too prevalent in recent days.

"Hi," I returned with a smile.

"Who are you?" he asked with a scrunched nose. His mother did that exact thing. It was cute.

"I am your mommy's boss."

"Liam is Mommy's boss," he responded.

"Hmm, yes." It didn't go lost on me that not only had he met Liam but knew him well enough to remember his name and who he was. "I am Mommy's other boss," I explained.

He shrugged his shoulders. "What are you doing here?"

"I have come to pick her up."

"Did you bring me anything?" he asked, tilting his head to the side.

I laughed internally. "No, I'm sorry, I did not. Is there anything in particular you want?"

"I want a puppy," he deadpanned.

"A puppy?" I asked. He nodded his head as the clicking of heels alerted the child to leave.

"Gotta go! Mommy's coming. Bye bye." He ran off.

"Bye bye," I waved with a laugh.

"Hey pumpkin, here you are. I've been looking for you. Mommy has to leave. You be good for Mrs. Santos, ok? I love you."

"I love you, Mommy."

The little feet rushed up the stairs. I turned around as Ava walked into the living room.

"Hi," she said, floating in, wearing a pink gown made of the lightest material, looking like the breeze had carried her in. This dress was very different from the last gown she wore. This one was soft and subtle, like a cloud. This was hers, all hers. This image was all Ava.

"Hi," I responded, unable to keep my eyes from grazing over her figure and unable to find my words. My legs seemed to be on autopilot, carrying me toward her until we were at arm's length.

"You look beautiful." I finally managed to get out a compliment. I noticed the pink flush of her cheeks. That was the thing about Ava, she couldn't take a compliment. She never could, not even as a teenager. I leisurely tucked a piece of her hair behind her ear.

"Thank you," she whispered.

I cleared my throat, taking a step back, realizing I was crowding her. "I was just greeted by your son."

"Oh goodness, yes, I see that. How did it go?" She asked.

"Brief," I answered. "He wanted to know who I am, what I am doing here. He also asked if I brought him anything."

Ava laughed. "Yep, that's him!" She ran her hand down her dress, smoothing out the fabric. "Should we go?"

"Yes, let's."

I walked ahead in the direction of my curb side parked car, while Ava lingered behind to lock her door. She stopped short upon reaching my car.

"What is this!" She exclaimed wide-eyed as she scanned the vehicle. I didn't understand what the problem was or what she was questioning. She read my puzzled look and furthered.

"What is this shoebox of a car? Where is the Porsche? How am I supposed to get into this car in this dress?"

"This car costs more than that house you are living in! It is hardly a shoebox."

"I mean because of the compact size," she clarified.

"Let me help you in." I gestured for her to come closer. I picked up the silky pink fabric of her dress and opened the passenger side door. She didn't have much room to move given the size of the door and she backed up into me. Her back was pressed against my chest and I couldn't say it bothered me. I rather liked having her that close. Her hair was inches from my face and her scent penetrated my senses, intoxicating me as always. I was done.

"Sorry," she apologized as her backside rubbed into my chest and I intentionally inhaled her scent as one would a swig of a cigarette.

"You smell good, Ava. What is that fragrance?"

She leaned to get in the car and once seated, she looked up at me with her 1,000-watt smile. The one that I rarely got anymore. "I can't tell you that. It's for me to know. It's my secret and I don't share."

"Shame, I was going to offer to get you the largest bottle available so I could be sure you smell like that every day at work. It would surely keep me on my feet." I closed her door and ran around to the other side.

"Guess you like your cars on the petite side," she said as I got in, adjusting my jacket. I laughed at her choice of words.

"Yes, I suppose. Petite like my women." She couldn't hide the blush my comment generated and I pressed on teasingly. "Be careful Ava, you are sounding more and more like you fit my mold."

"Fit your mold? Hardly, your women and cars may be petite but they have large assets," she said as she waved her hands about her chest area.

"I think your assets are perfectly suitable for my needs." Ava's face flushed with my response. We pulled away, heading toward the hills.

"So, what's his name?" I asked to change the subject. "Your son."

"Why do you ask?"

I laughed. "It's just a question, Ava. Relax! It's small talk. Don't you think I should know your kids' names if this is to look believable?"

She flipped her hair over her shoulder with an audible exhale. "My daughter is Melanie."

"Melanie, that's a pretty girl's name."

"Yeah, I think so," she nodded.

"And the boy?"

Ava oddly wasn't answering. I looked at her and I could see the wheels turning in her head. She was avoiding the question but I waited. We drove on in silence until she finally succumbed.

"Nicholas," she stated flatly. I turned my head so that she was in full view and I couldn't help the sly smile that took over my face.

"Excuse me?" I asked at a loss for words.

"My son's name is Nicholas."

I'll be dammed!

"That's a great boy's name," I obviously agreed, nodding my head, trying my hardest to hide the laugh that wanted to eagerly escape from my lips. And it wasn't a comical laugh, rather a personal satisfaction that I clearly had left an impression on her. Shit, she named her kid after me or so I wanted to believe.

"I understand now," I managed to add.

"What do you mean?" she asked unknowingly.

"I understand why you call me by my last name. It would be hard for you to think of me romantically if you called me by your son's name."

"We are not romantic," she stated emphatically.

"We could be," I added sincerely.

"We won't be."

I smiled at her and she smiled back. This back-and-forth teasing was fun. I could deal with this for a while longer.

"He wants a puppy," I told her.

"That sounds about right." She nodded, rolling her eyes. "He and his sister ask me every day for a puppy."

"Are you going to get them a puppy?" I asked. She vehemently shook her head at my question. "Oh, come on. Why not? Get the children what they want!" I joked.

"Nope. I don't take on more than I can handle and I am barely handling what I have." She pulled at a string on the hem of her dress. "I don't need something else to care for."

"Maybe you can lighten the load and let someone care for you."

"I can take care of myself," she stated with an exhale.

"Yes, we all can but you could let someone take care of you. We all need some help," I proposed before silence fell between us. She didn't respond or accept my remarks.

"Anyway, what's the game plan for tonight?" She finally spoke.

I don't know what prompted me, perhaps it was the shimmery smooth skin or the sun's rays that shone across her but I reached out and rubbed my hand on Ava's thigh. It seemed so inviting as it peeked out from behind the fabric. I felt her tense before I even touched her.

And just like that, with rocket speed reflexes, she swatted my hand away. I knew I was pushing the envelope but couldn't help myself and I smiled as I retreated.

"What do you mean, the plan?" I asked. "The plan is to be yourself. Just as you are."

"Oh, dear and how is that?"

I snickered at her restless inquiry. "I like you as you are. Maybe not like you are acting at this exact moment. Maybe you can pretend to enjoy my company a tad bit more," I admitted. Her reaction gave nothing away. She was perpetually hard to read.

"I hope you like me as I am," I added, hoping for more input from her. "At least you did when we were kids. Just pretend we are hanging out the same as then. No different from last Saturday night."

"That's a lot to ask for. Things are different now," she commented.

"They don't have to be, Ava. Just go with the flow. It shouldn't be that difficult."

Chapter 22
Ava

Nervousness took over as I accepted that I wasn't at all prepared. I was completely out of control in this matter and I didn't like to not be in control. Being out of control didn't serve me well in my marriage and I vowed when my husband left to never again be manipulated, influenced, limited or regulated. Nick threatened that vow, he threatened my clasp on control.

We were driving through the steep, winding roads that led up into the hills. The further up we went, the worse my uneasiness got. It felt like a time machine taking me back to a time I didn't want to return to.

The sun was now low as it got ready to set for the day. It cast rays that flickered between the branches of the eucalyptus and cypress tree. We drove higher up the twisty roads as Nick's sports car hugged the curves through the tight turns and quick stops brought on by his lead foot.

We had come to a red light and suddenly, Nick leaned over in my direction. His cologne ticked my sensations. His face was mere inches from mine due to the intimacy of his tiny sports car. I didn't turn to look at him. I knew he wanted me to but I wouldn't dare. I was afraid of what I would see or how I would react if I looked at him.

My stomach flipped in anxious anticipation as he grabbed my face gently with both his hands. His palms were warm and soft, as they gently guided me to look at him. His proximity made me instinctively move back away from him.

"What are you doing!" I exclaimed, my eyes searched his for an answer.

"I'm going to kiss you, Ava."

"What?" I exaggerated. "Closter, have you lost your mind?"

"No. That is what people who are intimate and like each other do."

"Let me remind you, we aren't either one of those things." I rolled my eyes and looked out the side window.

"No, we are not but it won't hurt if everyone else thinks we are. I don't want you to look surprised when we kiss, so I think we need to get this first kiss out of the way and maybe practice, so it looks natural."

I whipped my attention back in his direction. "You would like that, wouldn't you Closter?" He smirked and I waved my finger in his face. "I don't think so. It's not happening."

The light turned green, saving me from further explanation. He pressed on the accelerator as the car sped up a tight turn and I was abruptly thrown onto Nick's side of the car. I looked into his eyes, feeling embarrassed as my tummy fluttered at the raw desire that his eyes cast my way.

"I'm sorry," I swallowed hard. "You should slow down." I returned to my seat, adjusting my dress as I smoothed the fabric with my hands. He chuckled then we drove the rest of the way in silence.

We finally reached our destination. A stately stucco and stone building that looked a bit like a palace. It laid on the cliff overlooking the rocky side of the island. With the sun setting, it appeared that the surf down below was pounding into glowing orange diamonds that jetted out of the sea. I took in the view, all too aware that never in even a hundred years would I tire of the landscape of Vilamor.

We drove through an open black iron gate. Nick chose to not drive straight to the valet area but rather, he took the circle driveway beyond to park the car himself. It was strange to me that a man of his position and wealth didn't stop at the valet port but perhaps he didn't like having a stranger park his car.

He picked a secluded spot under an old olive tree. The view from here was spectacular. He sighed in an exaggerated manner while turning the car off and before I could gather myself to exit, he abruptly turned to me, clasping my face once more before crashing his lips to mine with the most unexpected kiss.

It was forceful at first, in a non-aggressive way and then became the sweetest and most tender physical moments I had ever shared with anyone in my life. It was frightening, shiver producing and electrifying. Something I never felt before. Something I never thought I would feel. Something I was sure was only written about in books but never actually attainable in reality.

Nick released me and straightened, returning to his side of the car. I watched in the most stunned way as he looked in the rear-view mirror and fixed his tie. He looked perfectly normal and unaffected as I watched him. I, on the other hand, was all sorts of frazzled.

"My apologies," he started, not bothering to turn my way, "but that had to be done."

He opened his door and walked out. He came around to my side of the car. I gave myself those few seconds to sit and process, trying to calm my racing heart. He opened my door and put out his hand to help me like a gentleman, only to then pull me closer. My chest bumped into his as he crowded my personal space once more. He lowered his divine face, finding my lips and kissed me again.

It was a solid kiss that made my head spin in the most glorious way and my weak knees wanted to give out. As if he could read my mind or interpret my body, he held me tighter so that I would not crumble. His gentle tongue found its way to mine, as if they were always destined to be together and it playfully teased, evocative of what more there could be between us.

My mind went clear. I saw light, bright light behind my closed eyelids. Glorious and splendid, I forgot myself, my circumstances, my worries, my concerns and who he was. The kiss left me eager for more and in a sweet daze. Then, just as abruptly as it started, he ended it, when he unexpectedly pulled away. My body trembled with the absence of his warmth.

We stood still and silent. We gazed at one another. Speechless. His lips were slightly parted and his eyes had gone from black coal to soft milk chocolate. I wanted to stay just like that forever.

His hand came up to catch a random lock of my hair. He rubbed it like ribbon between his fingers. Then smiling for reasons beyond me, he bowed his head, bringing his face closer to mine to whisper in my ear. I inhaled his tantalizing cologne that did all sorts of things to my insides.

"That was good, Ava but you have to get that deer in headlights look off your face." I swallowed hard and composed myself to gather my thoughts.

"How about next time you don't take me by surprise?" My eyes combed over his features, finally landing on his lips. "A little warning would be nice," I said in a whisper.

He straightened and started walking toward the venue, leaving me still bewildered with my feet planted firmly on the ground. "Where are you going?" I asked, disoriented.

"Into the party. Come on, we are late."

"What! Just like that?" I trotted behind him, trying to catch up with his long strides. "You kiss me like that and then walk away?"

"It was just a kiss, Ava. Get yourself together. Come on, we have a party full of people to impress."

"Can you at least wait up for me? I am walking in heels." He stopped abruptly, turning toward me as I collided into his chest. I took two steps back, needing the distance. He was looking above my head, gazing at the horizon beyond as he spoke slowly and with thought.

"My apologies. I am being rude," he paused, assessing his words. "It has been some time since I have done the dating thing."

He rubbed his lower lip with his thumb and then finally allowed himself to look down at me. "I will ask you for your patience while I learn."

I nodded, momentarily suspended in speechlessness. How could the womanizing Nicholas Closter, who was so arrogant and always so sure of himself be asking me, Ava Agostini, for patience while he 'learns' to do 'the dating thing'? I hadn't myself been on a date in twelve years. I sure as hell didn't know what I was doing either. He gave me his arm and I looped mine through.

"Thank you," I said, finding my voice.

"Of course."

We walked up the slight incline to the main entrance. "Why are you being so fidgety today?"

"Am I? Now you sound like Gina," I laughed. "I'm just nervous. It's our first appearance."

"It will be fine. You are with me." His thumb rubbed my hand reassuringly and I couldn't help but smile. "Come on."

This was a dream. An out of body experience and I had to admit I liked it. The kiss and everything about Nicholas was so delightful and I just didn't want to wake up from it. I knew this was all for pretend but I was here with him tonight and enjoying it.

He paused right before we entered the foyer, tugging lightly on my hand. "In case I haven't said it yet or if I forget to mention it," he paused to take a breath, "you look beautiful, Ava."

I smiled and I could feel the heat in my cheeks. "Yeah?" I questioned.

"Yeah. You took my breath away when you came down those stairs. You looked hot at the retirement party but tonight, tonight you look stunning."

"Thank you. You're pretty stunning too."

"Then we are in good company and will be the couple to envy. Come on before I kiss you again."

Chapter 23
Ava

Nick and I stepped into the ornate lobby, hand in hand. We looked around the awkwardly shaped rotunda with three long hallways that branched out from the center. The hallway straight ahead had an overly sized canvas of Christopher and Alana atop a black easel.

"That way," I said, pointing to the picture of the happy couple.

"Ah, yes," he said with raised eyebrows as he studied the excessively sexual engagement photo of Christopher and Alana. I watched him as his eyes then scanned from one hallway to the next as he turned about the room. "If their event is boring, we can always crash the other two."

I laughed, "I have a feeling we would be missed and noticed."

"Perhaps." Nick grabbed my hand in the same way he did all those years ago when we were kids but today it was different. It felt different as he took my hand to his lips and gave it a tender kiss. Such a simple gesture but his lips scorched my skin and they jolted my senses as my stomach muscles contracted no differently than they had decades before.

"Are you ready?" He asked me and all I could do was stupidly nod, unable to speak. "Ok, let's do this."

We walked hand in hand, his completely wrapping around my smaller hand in a way that gave me a sense of security. Our steps were synced and our heads held high as we both stepped toward what we knew was a lion's den of gossip.

We knew there would be talk of us arriving together. We knew there would be glances. We knew this would be the beginning of a new slew of gossip. There was no turning back now and I didn't want to turn back. I preferred this gossip to any that had existed about me in the past.

That of the jilted assistant, which was exactly what most assumed after Liam's recent engagement. Or worse yet, the gossip of my husband; where he was, was I a widow, what happened to him, how I became a single mom, etc. I had heard it all and being on Nick's arm was the better option.

At least with Nick, people didn't avoid me like the plague. They had done just that back in New York when my husband left and I saw the same look in people's eyes after Liam's engagement.

We stepped through the threshold, into the event space and as expected, heads turned. It didn't help that we were late but I think this was exactly how Nick wanted it to go.

"Nicholas!" A woman's voice shrieked above the rumble of the party. We both turned simultaneously in the direction of Nick's aunt Debra, Luke's mother. She grabbed Nick's face and brought it down to her lips as she kissed his forehead.

"What kind of a nephew comes back to town weeks ago and doesn't stop at his favorite aunt's house?"

"My only aunt," Nick said, clearing his throat.

"Yes but favorite all the same."

"Yes, my favorite," Nick admitted, hugging his aunt. Nick stood almost two heads taller than her petite frame. "I've missed you, Aunt Debra," he said, squeezing her a little tighter. "I'm sorry. It has been a wild few weeks since my return and I didn't want to give you a half assed visit."

"Hmmm, ok, lucky for you, I am forgiving. But you'll come by one of these Sundays for family dinner, yes?" She fidgeted with his already perfect tie.

"Yes, of course." Nick turned his gaze my way and grabbed my hand, pulling me closer. "Auntie, do you know Ava?"

"Do I know Ava?" she asked sarcastically. "Of course, I do, I feel like I know her better than I know you. Ava is family now. Isn't that so?"

I shook my head. "Yes. Your aunt Debra has been very good to me." I smiled at her.

"You both came together?" Her eyes floated between Nick and me but she didn't wait for an answer. "You treat her well, Nicholas. Do you hear me? She isn't a floosy like some of those other girls you've brought around. Holy! Too many to count!"

"Ok, Aunt Debra!" Nick rapidly added, to quiet her. "No worries. I have no intentions of mistreating her." He squeezed my hand and my pulse quickened.

"Aunt Debra," he tilted his head. "Don't you have sons to go bother or guests to greet?"

"Trying to rush me along, are you? You are a son too, so it's my duty to bother you. It is how your mother would want it. But yes, I suppose I should mingle. Table arrangements are there," she said, pointing to a round table, "but regardless, you are at Luke and Gina's table."

She gave Nick a kiss on the cheek, having to stand on her toes to do so, then turned, giving me a hug. "Ok kids, go have some fun."

"Well, your aunt certainly called you out?" I said jokingly after she was out of ears reach.

"Yes. I am ashamed. I should have visited her. My mother would be disappointed," he stated flatly and as I watched him; I saw what I thought was a melancholy sadness wash over his face.

"Hey!" Greeted Luke, overly enthusiastic as usual, while he patted Nick on the back.

"Hey, how are you guys?"

"We are great! Ava, you look beautiful!"

"Thank you."

"We are over here." Luke directed Nick ahead and I stayed behind with Gina.

"Well, well, you came with Nicholas Closter?" Gina arched her brow as she looked me over. "Gorgeous dress by the way."

"Thanks. Yours too."

"So, anything you want to tell me?" she asked, cutting to the chase.

I wasn't ready to answer questions. I didn't think about the questions that would arise, especially from anyone that knew me as personally as Gina.

"Just kidding." She smiled. "Luke told me everything."

"He told you?" I questioned with relief.

"Yes, all of it!"

"Oh, thank God! I didn't know what to say and I didn't want to lie to you."

"Yep! He told me. I just don't understand." She shook her head, squinting her eyes and puckering her lips. "I know why Nick suggested it but for the life of me, I don't understand why you agreed to this silly arrangement."

I shrugged my shoulders, not having an answer to give her.

"Is it because you want Liam?" She inquired. "Or is it because you want Nick?"

"What?" I gasped. "Don't be absurd, Gina." I shook my head but avoided eye contact with her.

"Then why? What are your reasons?" She moved about me to the other side so that I had no choice but to look at her.

"I don't know." I sighed, shrugging my shoulders. I really didn't know the answer to her question. "I guess because I don't want Liam to make a lifelong mistake and maybe I am curious what would have happened if he had returned unattached. I don't know."

"Is that what you are telling yourself?"

"Yes, what else would it be? Gina, what are you getting at?" I asked, annoyed.

"Oh, I don't know," she said, moving a lock of my hair, the same lock of hair that Nick played with before. "After hearing you and Nick tell the story of how you met, I was skeptical if this was a way to see what it would be like to date him. You know, a bit of an experiment." She patted my cheek and I knew exactly what she was doing. She was trying to get into my head by invading my personal space.

"Don't be ridiculous, Gina. That was decades ago. We were kids and nothing happened."

"Right. Exactly. Nothing happened. Aren't you the least bit curious what could have happened?"

I could feel my cheeks turn red under her cross examination. The warmth was clouding my thoughts.

"No," I responded blandly. "Being the topic of this gossip is better than being the topic of other gossip." I played with my earring, a nervous gesture I had since childhood. "That is the reason and should be reason enough."

"Ok! Whatever." She moved her hand in a dismissive manner. "Come on, let's grab our seats, I am starving."

Gina clutched my hand and walked me toward our table that was obnoxiously placed in front of the DJ set up. Luke and Nick were already drinking and talking tete-a-tete as the melody of the music filled the atmosphere.

I observed as Luke was at Nick's ear, clearly doing all the talking but Nick wasn't paying attention to him. Instead, he was watching me and he didn't hide it. He didn't hesitate to look my way and even smiled as I approached. It was uncanny how he could always sense my presence as if he had an internal radar.

I watched him and as I did, I found Gina's words repeating through my head, suddenly knocking the wind out of me. My God! The realization sent tremors through my body. Why did I agree to this? Maybe, just maybe, Gina was right. A small part of me was in fact curious what would have happened if Nick and I had stayed in contact. How would my life be different now?

Would I have stayed in Vilamor? Would he have stayed in Vilamor? Would he and I have had a relationship? Would he have been the father of my children? Would we still be together? Would we be happy and in love?

Those thoughts, those questions, all the would haves and could haves and many more ran through my mind as I stared at the staggering, extraordinary being that was Nicholas Closter.

"Here," interrupted Gina with a nudge. "I took the liberty of ordering you a Pina colada and me, a virgin. I know, strange drink to order but I was craving coconut. So weird, right?" She handed me the glass as the robust coconut aroma surrounded me and transported me to a time and place long, long ago.

Vilamor-August 2000

Nick picked me up in his Vespa, as usual, and we went to the marina. Our legs hung over the limestone pier while my skin sizzled in the heat from basking in the bright afternoon sun. I flinched as the feeling of cold lotion slid down my shoulder. The beachy smell of coconut was strong as Nick's large hands lathered the creamy, white sunscreen on my shoulders and down my back.

My skin cooled as his hands gently dragged the silky lotion. He was the first person of the male gender to ever rub sunscreen on me or even touch me for that matter. I tried to act cool, aloof and unaffected but the goose bumps along my arms betrayed me as they revealed the truth.

"There. That should help," he said, clearing his throat as he closed the tube of sunscreen and threw it onto his black backpack. "You are way too fair to be out here without protection."

"Thank you. Taking care of me as usual," I said, elbowing him lightly.

"Someone needs to," he replied flatly.

"Sure. And should I take care of you?" I smirked.

"I think that is a fair compromise." His lips moved upward, revealing his striking smile as he moved a strand of my hair behind my ear. "I'll take care of you and you take care of me."

He put out his hand and we shook.

A ball of feelings filled my chest and cut off my air supply as the memory replayed in my mind. I hated going back to those times. I had blocked those memories for so long and now lately, they all seemed to flutter back.

Oh, my dear God, what had I gotten myself into? I clutched my chest, reminding myself to breathe. I gasped for air. I couldn't fall for this man. I couldn't allow it. Surely it was just Gina getting in my head. Surely it would pass.

These were all just senseless thoughts. Nicholas Closter didn't do relationships. He didn't like children. This would never have been and it never could be.

"Hello? Knock, knock. Earth to Ava." Gina's voice sounded hollow as she mock knocked me on my head.

Her voice shook me back to my current reality. I blinked repeatedly as I continued staring ahead at Nick. His brows furrowed with concern and he silently mouthed to me across the way. I read his lips, "Are you alright?" they questioned. Without thought or hesitation, I nodded yes and broke our intent gaze as I turned to address Gina.

"I'm sorry. You said something?" I asked her.

"Wow!" She exclaimed, wide eyed. "Where were you just now because you certainly weren't here?"

"Umm, I think I'm just hungry. I haven't really eaten much all day," I reassured her.

"Nick, Nick to the rescue!" Gina called out dramatically. "Get your girl some food before she passes out."

Nick's girl? Ha! That wouldn't happen. It couldn't happen. Ever. I couldn't let it.

Chapter 24
Ava

Most of the evening was uneventful. Honestly, I preferred it that way. I'm not much for theatrics or drama. Tonight was the usual, run of the mill engagement party; congratulatory speeches, lots of kisses from the happy couple and plenty of food, as would our cultures ever allow for anything less.

For the most part, Nick and Luke spent the evening engaged in conversation with anyone and everyone that approached the table. It was rather comical as it often appeared to resemble an assembly line. Guest upon guest made their way over to congratulate Luke and Gina on their pregnancy and would then inevitably stroll over to Nick.

He had been gone for so long that he seemed an apparition. Most knew him from either his youth, his family association or from the business word. They wanted to exchange words, any words, with Nicholas Closter and as I watched him work his charm, I understood why. His charisma was, in fact, contagious and appealing.

With all this though, he never let me go too far. He hung his arm over my shoulder protectively and possessively while often adorning my forehead with kisses. But it was the gentle knee and thigh rubs that made me wince in my seat. Sure, this was all for show, for him but I hadn't been touched in years.

He rested his elbow over the back of my chair, leaning into my personal space. "Luke caught me touching the goods," he breathed into my ear. I pushed away to study his face, puzzled by his statement.

"I'm sorry, I'm not following—"

"That's how he worded it. He said I touched the good," he chuckled. "I was wearing evidence, he said. You could have warned me our kisses left lip gloss on my lips."

"Oh!" I squeezed my eyes shut in regret. "I didn't notice. I'm sorry. I think I was in too much of a daze to notice."

"Well, the cat is out of the bag and knowing Luke, Gina will know by the end of the evening."

"I'm sorry."

"Don't be! I wouldn't want it any other way. I want everyone here to know, without question, that you are with me," he winked. "Don't go too far. I'll be back."

To say that I was relieved when he and the other men went outside for cigars would be an understatement. This was all fantastic, foreign and frightening. I don't know if it was the Pina Colada or the white wine but I suddenly felt all warm and content inside. I was also extremely sexually triggered and needed breathing space.

The table was now vacant and I took the opportunity to leave and use the restroom to clear my head. I walked mindlessly, looking for a restroom. I found one, a rather lavish, substantially sized woman's bathroom suite near the main foyer.

I ventured around the halls, peeking into the other venue rooms. I didn't often attend functions and curiosity called me. It was comical how one room was a rowdy wedding and the other a more conservative 50th wedding anniversary.

I was on my way back to Chris and Alanna's party when I was grabbed from behind into an empty bar room. The room was colder and darker compared to the hallway and my eyes were fighting to adjust to the lack of light. The cold sent shivers through my body.

I wanted to scream as fear filled me but a man's hand covered my mouth, making it impossible. I tried to shout but as I did, I felt the familiar body behind me and an equally familiar voice at my ear.

"Shh," the voice whispered. The hairs on the back of my neck stood as I became aware it was Liam. What was he doing? He turned me around in his arms.

"Don't make any loud noise. There are people on the terrace right outside that door," he cradled me in his arms.

"Liam? What are you doing here? Shouldn't you be with Samantha?" I responded, examining his dark eyes and face that were contoured by shadows.

"She's four champagnes in. She's fine."

"Liam, we shouldn't be in here, someone might see us together," I explained but he only shrugged uninterested in my words, so I furthered. "Your brother might see us," I said, purposely mentioning Nick, hoping that in doing so he would let me go.

"Let him! I don't care!" He spilled the words in such an animated manner that his neatly combed hair flopped toward his forehead. "I need to see you. I need to talk to you."

I pushed from his embrace and scurried to the other side of the room. "I don't think we have anything to talk about, Liam."

"I miss you," he said, taking long strides closer to me. "I really miss you, Ava. You must miss me too? Don't you?" He placed his hand under my chin. "Please look at me, just tell me that you do."

"Have you lost your mind?" I asked. "Liam, you are engaged."

"Maybe I have. I just need to know. I need to know, please just answer my question, my one question."

"We don't have anything to talk about, Liam. I am very happy for you and Samantha."

He took two steps closer and grabbed my arms.

"Please don't say her name anymore. I don't want to talk about Samantha or my engagement." His eyes scoured over my face and his grasp tightened around my upper arms to the point where it was no longer comfortable. How different his touch was compared to his brother's touch.

"I want to know, what are you doing with my brother?" He questioned, pulling me closer, in an awkwardly painful manner. "Are you seeing him?" He asked. I could smell the liquor on his breath. The smell of intoxication was becoming a habit for him.

***

Nicholas

The salty breeze picked up as day was now night. I stood outside on the terrace, smoking a cigar surrounded by acquaintances, old and new. But I felt lonely. I wished Ava was out here with me. How quickly she had gotten back under my skin.

As I looked around, I ached to see her, knowing she would love this view. And there my mind went again! Always back to Ava, like a compass seeking true north.

"Another?" asked Luke, holding out a bottle of scotch in my direction.

I shook my head. I had been out here for a while. I lost track of how long but every cell of my being told me it was long enough. Luke splurged on the cigars and he refused no for an answer. He insisted we all stayed to enjoy the camaraderie. That was Luke for you. He always was the center of the party, insisting upon only good times and good conversation. That's why we all loved him.

The men, mostly cousins of mine, close and distant, enjoyed some laughs and reminiscing banter. It was fine and even enjoyable except for my brother's presence and his seeping hatred toward me, which I was sure made all the guys equally as uncomfortable as I was.

Liam made no attempts to hide his animosity. At least being outside with him allowed me to keep an eye on him. We hadn't yet exchanged words this evening or even any pleasantries for that matter. I didn't mind it. I didn't need to have a close relationship with my brother. I had gone this long without it.

Liam was smooth and I almost didn't notice his escape. He quietly went back inside but I did eventually notice his lack of presence and knowing how his mind worked, I set out to find Ava. She had been gone from me for far too long.

I knew she could handle her own but I was missing her. I was ashamed to admit it but I wanted to bask in her company. I wanted to enjoy her smile, take in her laugh and breathe in her scent. I enjoyed her company far more than I enjoy most people.

I had done this evening what I had wanted to do for so long. I dreamed, fantasized, obsessed over what it would be like to kiss Ava. To kiss my Frankie. I was floating; invigorated tonight as the kiss, the taste of Ava and the feeling of holding her hadn't disappointed. Just the opposite. It was as glorious as I had hoped.

I had exhausted years fixating and truly believing I had lost my opportunity. Then, to have it again. The problem now was I liked it too much. I liked her company, her laugh, her smile, her scent, her kiss too much and didn't want to think about letting it go. Tonight, for now, I just wanted to continue living in this blissful afterglow.

I left the terrace, left the men and the cigars and went out searching. I went toward the restrooms, not that I could or would barge in but I stood outside and waited until a familiar face came out.

"Hey, peeping Tom, what are you doing here?"

"Gina. Are you going in?" I asked, pointing toward the bathroom door.

"Of course, I am, what do you think? I'm pregnant, this is my third visit already."

"Could you do me a favor and see if Ava is in there? She's been gone for a while. I just want to make sure she's ok."

"Oh, sure. Now that you mention it, I haven't seen her around either. Let me go in and check, I'll be right out."

I leaned against the cold wall, watched and waited impatiently until Gina popped her head out. "She's not here. I'll help you look for her but I really need to go to the bathroom first."

"Nah, don't worry about it, I got it."

I pulled away from the wall and looked down the long hall. Where could she have gone? I walked toward the coat room but she was nowhere to be seen. I had just about given up my search and was headed back to our table when I became aware of voices coming from a darkened room. I pushed the ajar door and upon adjusting my eyesight, I just about lost my head when my eyes settled upon Ava in Liam's embrace.

They both instantly turned their heads toward me at the realization of my presence. I first noticed Ava's pale face and then the look of relief in her eyes.

"Nick!" She exclaimed in an exasperated tone.

I flipped out. My view went red as I saw how Liam held Ava. I didn't like it. I didn't like how he held her or even the fact that he was that close to her.

"What's going on in here?" I demanded.

"Nick, it's not what you think," pled Ava, her head nodding vigorously.

My legs carried me forward and I was at her side before I knew it. I pulled her hand to get her away from Liam.

"I'm not sure what it looks like!" I responded. "It doesn't look good!"

My eyes examined her and I saw red marks on her arms. I instantly, mentally questioned how tightly Liam had been holding her or why he held her that way. I turned my attention to my brother, seeing nothing but red.

"Let this be a warning, Liam," I spewed, "keep your hands off Ava."

"Shouldn't that be up to her?" He countered.

"It isn't a request, Liam! It's a warning. I won't be as gentle hearted with regards to Ava as I have been about Samantha. You like my seconds; obviously. You can have Samantha but you leave Ava the hell alone."

I pulled Ava closer, then turning, I walked her out of that room and straight out of that building. I walked and kept walking. I lost my manners. I lost my senses. I didn't care that there was a room full of expectant people that would notice our absence. I just knew at that moment that I needed or better yet, wanted to get Ava away from Liam.

The walk to the car remained quiet. Ava didn't speak and I was too absorbed in my rage to speak. Although, I noticed her deep breathing and her shaking hands. She was nervous, anxious or afraid. I did hope she wasn't afraid of me. I was furious. I could acknowledge my fury but never did I want to spark fear in her.

I needed air and needed to get the image of Ava in Liam's arms out of my head. I didn't like how I was reacting. I didn't like how Ava had gotten into my head. I was infuriated with Liam. I was frustrated with Ava and I was disappointed with myself for my reaction.

"What did he say to you?" I finally asked, once we were both in the confines of the car.

"Only that he wanted to talk to me," her voice was low and quivered. "He said that he missed me."

"And?" I knew there was more and I questioned her for it.

"And he asked what is going on between us."

"What did you say?"

"Nothing," she exhaled. "That's when you walked in."

We drove in silence. The drive home took much longer than I remembered. I allowed the silence to remain between us, worried that if I spoke further, I would take my rage and pain out on her or be too aggressive.

I pulled up to her house and put the car in park, finally breathing. I didn't want her to leave like this. I rested my head on the headrest and concentrated on my breathing. I tried to rid myself of the temper that burned inside. Ava shuffled at my side, gathering her belongings to leave.

"Have a good night," she spoke with her hand clutching the door handle, ready to leave me. I didn't want to let her go. I wanted her to stay. I wanted her to go home with me. I wanted her to remain with me forever. I placed my hand on her leg to pause her.

"Ava, let's not let this be how we end the night," I spoke to the back of her head, hoping she would turn. I wanted to see her eyes, I wanted to connect with her again.

"It's fine, Closter. We don't have to talk about it. You don't have to explain and neither do I." She turned and the look in her eyes dismissed me. "Go home. I'll see you Monday." She was done. I knew it by her tone and knew it by the way she went back to calling me by my surname.

"Yes." I studied her face. I searched her features to decipher if it was pain, anger or both. "Monday then," I responded, knowing there was little to nothing I could do to salvage the night. "Good night, Ava."

Chapter 25
Nicholas

The following day was a hungover, dazed and emotionally empty mess. It was a painful Sunday to get through. I wasn't an admirer of weekends to begin with. I didn't enjoy having time to myself. I needed purpose and I only had it at work.

I hated how things had ended last night. It was the best day of my life, because I finally kissed Ava but also the worst because of how I felt today. It irked me in all sorts of ways that I could not explain. Ava and I had been getting close. We had connected, I was sure of it and it now felt that we had taken steps back.

That night, I laid in bed reliving our conversations and the memory of the way she felt when I kissed her. The memory overwhelmed me endlessly. I knew as soon as I pulled away from her kiss that I was done. There was no going back. I replayed it over and over.

I ran from that kiss as soon as I could regain enough strength to do so. I fled toward the venue to escape her and give myself much needed distance. I couldn't have her look into my eyes; if she had, she would have been privy to the shocking longing that they would reveal. I hadn't ever felt that way. I wasn't ready for it and she certainly wouldn't welcome it.

As I lay there in bed with my insomnia, I became aware that I was doomed. This was uncharted territory for me. I was totally obsessed with her. It was no longer just about the Laurent acquisition. And it dawned on me that perhaps it never had been.

After hours of tossing, turning and lack of sleep, I decided to head into work early. I walked through the revolving glass doors into the lobby of Closter Enterprises. It was quiet, overly quiet and I reminded myself that it was still dawn.

"Good morning, Mr. Closter."

I turned my head toward the voice coming from the security desk. It was the guard that had watched Ava's kids the day she returned for the Laurent file. I walked, nearing the security desk.

"George, right?" I asked, tapping my hand on the marble countertop.

"Yes, sir."

"Good morning, George." He nodded his head in acknowledgment. "Quiet this morning, isn't it?"

"Yes, sir. It is my favorite time of the day, sir."

"Is that so?" He nodded. "Are you a morning person, George?"

"I am. I like the silence and the cool morning air. It's refreshing."

"I believe you are friendly with my assistant, Ava?"

"Yes, sir. She is a sweetheart. It would be difficult not to be friendly with her," he said with a smile.

"Yes, I can see that."

"She brings me coffee and breakfast some mornings without me even asking. It means more to me than she understands. You know, the night shifts can be hard to get through. There's nothing like a fresh cup of coffee and a pastry to keep me going until my shift is over."

"She does that?" I asked, registering his words.

"Yes."

I nodded, meditating over George's words. Ava was, in fact, a sweetheart. She had only shown me kindness, hard work and respect. I, on the other hand, had not been so respectful. I didn't deserve her or her affection. I knew I didn't but it didn't keep me from wanting to fight for it.

"Alright then. Well, thank you for your service, George." I nodded and turned back in the direction of the elevators.

I spent the next few hours trying to keep my mind distracted off Saturday, Ava and Liam but found it nearly impossible. To my relief, 9:00 a.m. was soon upon me and I had my scheduled meeting with Luke to occupy my mind. Time with my cousin always made things better.

As we both sat at my desk reviewing agendas, contracts and timelines, we were interrupted by a knock at the door as Ava arrived with my coffee and mail. She looked meek this morning. Dressed in a simple black knee length dress. She quietly placed the coffee on my desk and the mail in my tray as per usual.

"Good morning, Luke," she said, smiling at my cousin but didn't acknowledge me. She left just as gently as she had come in, leaving an unsettling atmosphere in the room, which Luke didn't let go unnoticed.

"Ok, out with it," he said. "What happened to you and Ava Saturday night? Last I saw you, we were outside smoking a cigar and then you disappeared."

I tapped my fingers on my desk, unsure of how much I wanted to tell him. "I found her and Liam talking, cohorting in an empty lounge area."

"Is that so?"

I nodded. "I didn't like it," I admitted. "I lost my cool, grabbed her and we left."

"Let me get this straight, you got a reaction from your brother, which is exactly what you wanted but you didn't like it?" I nodded at his question. "It seems this little charade between you and Ava is becoming more than a charade," he suggested.

"I didn't like the idea that someone else might see them. I know I need Liam and Samantha to split but I don't need Ava and Liam making me look like a fool. Anyone could have seen them, just as I had."

"Did you talk to Ava about it?"

"Yeah, she said she was returning from the restroom and he pulled her in."

"Ava won't make a fool of you."

"Yeah, I hope you are right. I don't know. I messed up. I wasn't taking it out on her but I think it may have come across that way. I wasn't thinking straight. I just saw red."

"Oh boy, Nick. I guess we are back to you and Ava being on the outs."

I didn't answer him but I knew he was right.

"What are you going to do?"

"You're asking me!" I exclaimed. "I don't know. I don't do well with this sort of thing. This is precisely why I don't do relationships."

"Well, it isn't really a relationship, right. It's a work thing, so deal with it as you would with anything work related."

"That's a good suggestion."

"Yeah, so what would Nicholas Closter do if there was a bump in the road with a new client or business associate?" I was catching on to what he was suggesting.

"Ok, I got you."

"Yeah, so turn on that Closter charm. Wine and dine her like you would a new acquisition."

And that was a good idea. That I could do. I grabbed my phone and opened the messaging app, finding her contact as I started typing.

Me: *Dinner tonight?*

I put my phone down and Luke watched me with his head in his hands.

"What?" I asked.

"Did you just text her?"

"Yeah, why?"

"You didn't even wait for me to leave. You have it bad for her," he said with a sly smile.

"Dude, you want me to fix this or not?" I picked up my phone and looked at the message. It was delivered and read but she hadn't responded. Was she laughing at my invitation? Was she considering it and smiling?

"Why isn't she responding?"

"Wow, yeah, you definitely have it bad! Give the girl a chance to read the message."

"She has read it!" I said out loud as I stared at the phone again. I was hopeful, anxious and curious as to what she would respond. Damn, she was plaguing my mind in a way I didn't understand. Was she aware of how much power she had over me?

Was that why she had me waiting? I rubbed my chin, unsure what to do with my jitters. Then they appeared, three small dots bounced across the screen. She was typing. Then my phone vibrated.

Ms. Agostini: *I can't.*

I assaulted my phone. Typing out quickly.

Me: *Why?*

Ms. Agostini: *Kids.*

Me: *Kids?*

Ms. Agostini: *Yes, my kids. I can't just leave them home alone.*

"What's going on? What did she write?" asked Luke, tapping his fingers impatiently on my desk.

"I asked her to dinner tonight. She said she can't because of the kids."

Luke rubbed his chin in thought. "Listen, I'll talk to Gina. We will take the kids if you promise to admit your undying love for Ava." He chuckled with a smart ass look on his face.

"Stop being stupid," I snapped.

He laughed. "We'll see who the stupid one is. Anyway, text her, let her know."

Me: *Luke says he and Gina will take the kids.*

Ms. Agostini: *I don't know. I didn't tell the kids. What is this dinner for anyway?*

"She is unsure," I told Luke. "She says she didn't tell her kids."

"Tell her the kids like me better than her and they will be thrilled to see me at pick up." He laughed. "Let me text Gina and let her know what's going on."

Me: *Luke says and I quote, "The kids like me better than her and will be thrilled to see me at pick up."*

Ms. Agostini: *Ugh. He's going to pick them up?*

Me: *Him and Gina. Come on, live a little. Have some fun.*

Ms. Agostini: *I feel bad, I have left them so often lately with all these events.*

Me: *Yes and my understanding is you've been inseparable for close to three years. It is one dinner, Ava.*

I watched as the three dots appeared and disappeared as she repeatedly started to type. It gave me hope. It meant she was considering it. Then finally.

Ms. Agostini: *Ok.*

A short, simple word but it brought me so much joy.

Me: *Ok?*

Ms. Agostini: *Yes. Ok, I'll have dinner with you.*

"She said yes!" I said, overly excited.

"Wow! This is the happiest I have seen you in forever, cousin. Glad Gina and I could make it happen. So, where are you taking her?"

I thought about it but nothing felt right.

"I don't want to have this conversation in a crowded restaurant."

"Right. I can understand that. How about your house?"

"My house?"

"Yeah, get takeout or something."

"Good idea."

"Yeah, I try."

"Half a good idea anyway. Hey, do you know where I can rent a Vespa?"

"What? Please tell me that you, mister 'I only drive cars with big price tags' is not going to rent a Vespa to pick up his date."

“I most definitely am renting a Vespa.”

“And you are telling me you aren’t ready to admit your undying love for her?”

“It isn’t love, Luke.”

“In that case, please put my mind to rest and tell me I am not aiding and abetting in your pursuit of seducing my wife’s cousin.”

“No worries, nothing will happen.”

“In that case, the surf shop down by Pearl Nightclub rents Vespas.”

“Cool, I’ve got some calls and planning to do. Go set up your part with Gina.”

“Will do but we are leaving early.”

“Yeah, that’s fine. Hell, the whole office can leave early today.”

“You really have lost it,” he professed, shaking his head.

“Make the announcement. Everyone can leave at lunchtime. It will be good for morale.”

“I like this Nicholas Closter better. How can we keep him around?”

Chapter 26
Ava

"Oh, my goodness!" I screamed with my hands on my hips. "You own a Vespa?" I was unable to contain my excitement as I opened my front door and saw the bright, shiny, red Vespa that was parked in my driveway.

"Hi!" Nick greeted me with the biggest smile, it warmed my insides. He was more handsome now in his 40s than he was in his youth, if that was even possible. "No, I don't own a Vespa. I'm a 40-year-old executive."

"You mean 41-year-old executive but who's counting, right?" I winked.

"You get the point."

"It seems every time you come to see me, you have a different mode of transportation," I stated.

"That seems about right. Some you have liked and some you have not. Can I assume you like the Vespa?"

"Yes, you can assume," I said, shrugging my shoulders.

"I rented it for old times' sake," he said, looking back at the Vespa, pleased with himself.

"I'm glad you got here in one piece."

"I did and I'll get you to our destination in one piece too."

I scrunched my nose at the odd fear I had of getting back on a Vespa after all these years. I hadn't been on one since I was 16.

"Oh, no worries, Vespas' are easy to ride," he continued. "Once you ride a Vespa, you never forget."

"Hmm."

"I thought it would be fun to see Vilamor and ourselves through old eyes."

"Is Nicholas Closter calling me old?" I joked.

"Never!" He laughed.

"For today, let's just forget who we are or are supposed to be. Tonight, you are just Ava, not a mom and I'm just Nick, not your boss." His hands clasped mine and I liked how that felt. I liked it too much.

"I don't even know who Ava is anymore," I confessed.

"Maybe the Vespa will remind you."

"Maybe."

His eyes roamed over me. "You look terrific."

"Thanks! I dressed as you suggested." I turned to show off my jean cut-off shorts and white top. "You had said to dress casually like when we were kids. So, I brought Y2K back and did one better."

We both laughed. "This is definitely Y2K. It is almost exactly what you wore the day we met." He smiled as I spun around again and my heart leaped with excitement that he remembered.

"I like it. It's perfect," he said, giving me two thumbs up.

"Good, I'm glad you like it."

We stood staring at one another, unsure of the next step. I watched his movements as he rubbed his ear. "I was nervous picking you up," he confessed.

"Were you?" I squinted in disbelief. "Why?"

"You were cold this morning," he stated, wide eyed.

"Was I?" Geez, had I been that cold? I hadn't given it much thought. It wasn't that I wanted to be cold but he wasn't exactly emitting the best vibes since Saturday night.

He nodded. "Just a bit," he responded, holding up his thumb and index finger together. "In fact, Luke was concerned."

"Luke is always concerned!" I rolled my eyes. "He wants everyone to always be in the best mood and get along all the time."

"That he does. Regardless, it appears you are in a better mood. I think the Vespa is paying off."

"Perhaps. So, are we going to stand here and talk about the Vespa or are we going to take it for a ride?" I asked.

"Of course! I rented it for 24 hours. We can ride as much as you want. My dear, your ride awaits," he gestured with his hands for me to go ahead of him.

I was hesitant but instinctively got on the Vespa right behind Nick. All fears were thrown to the wind. It felt just like old times as we rode through the winding roads of Vilamor on the shiny red Vespa. The hands of time had gone backward.

For the first time in countless years, I felt alive and untroubled. Really alive, in a way I hadn't noticed was missing. I felt my blood swim through my veins and my heart was pounding in my chest full of excitement. There were no worries, no concerns or thoughts in my mind as we zipped down toward the coast.

My arms unconsciously wrapped around Nick's welcoming, solid abdomen. My palms settled on his torso and I was stunned by how much harder he was then I remembered. The heat from his body scorched my skin but I liked it.

My stomach fluttered as my legs grazed against his, sending a tremor through my body. I let my head rest on his shoulder as I took in the views of our beautiful Vilamor. I felt safe. I didn't understand it. Nick had only just recently returned to my life but I felt more myself and safer than I ever had with my husband.

The warm breeze blew past me, taking with it all my troubles and I let my body relax against his. It felt good, no matter how briefly, to feel young again. Soon, much too soon, we were down by the shore. We stopped at a red light and Nick's hand tapped my bare thigh as he turned his head back toward me.

"Are you ok back there?" He asked with a grin.

"I'm better than ok," I responded, "I'm great!" I exclaimed, wishing his hand would stay on my thigh a little longer.

"Yeah. That you are," he replied and turned his focus back to the road as we merged into traffic heading down the main avenue along the sea.

We first stopped at a sandwich shop to buy paninis and seltzer waters, just like we did as kids. Then we went to the end of the pier, letting our legs dangle over the edge as we took in the view and watched the boats. The scene was set just as it had been twenty-two years ago. All that was missing was coconut scented sunscreen.

"What was the urgency with today's get together?" I asked between chews, succumbing to my curiosity.

"I didn't like how things were left Saturday," he countered. "I want to apologize. I need to apologize."

"You don't have to apologize. There isn't anything for you to apologize for."

"I do. I was wrong to take my anger out on you." He took the bottle of seltzer to his lips and took a brief sip. "It was disrespectful." Our eyes met and so many unspoken words were said with just one look.

"I also need to apologize for kissing you. I shouldn't have. Don't get me wrong, I wanted to. I still want to but I shouldn't have without your permission." I watched his lips as they thinned over his gleaming white teeth into a smile that beckoned me.

"Don't apologize. I didn't mind it," I admitted.

"You didn't?" he asked with squinted eyes, his face taking on a serious appearance.

I shook my head. "No. I wanted it as much as you."

"It was a good kiss, wasn't it?" His question brought on a blush that heated my core. I studied his mood as he looked out to the sea. "Do you remember this pier?" He asked.

"Of course, I do. This is the same spot we sat at on our last day together."

"Yep, 22 years ago. The day before you went missing from my life," his voice was somber.

I leaned back, resting my weight on the palms of my hands, letting the sun bathe me with its warmth. The sky was on fire with reds, pinks and corals as the sun rested. I watched as a pair of birds flew overhead, gliding opposite and then coming together.

Nick cleared his throat as he put down his bottle of seltzer and pulled his cell phone out of his pocket. He turned, pointing his phone at me and snapped a photo.

"Just. Like. That," he uttered, biting his bottom lip with a smile. "Thank you for that. This is exactly how I have remembered you," he continued watching me. "All these years, Ava. I have remembered you exactly like this, lounging in the afterglow of the sunset. The warm red sun glistening on your skin, sparkling in your eyes and shining in your hair." He looked at his phone before putting it in his pocket. He winked at me with a smile.

"You've thought about me over the years?" I asked, astonished by the awareness of his revelation.

"All the time," he confirmed, nodding his head.

He palmed my face, rubbing his thumb across my cheek as his body wandered closer. I knew the expression in his eyes. I knew he wanted to kiss me because I wanted it too.

"To answer your question from before, yes, it was a good kiss. The best," I said.

"It was," he agreed. "Maybe we could repeat it a few more times."

"I was thinking that too," I replied.

He shifted his weight closer to me, taking my face with both his hands.

"I can't tell you how many times I thought about kissing you. Kissing Frankie. Every day that summer I would pick you up and I'd chicken out every single time." We both laughed. "Don't take this the wrong way but I fantasized about it," he said honestly.

"You don't have to fantasize today."

He rubbed his thumb over my bottom lip and smiled. I stared into his eyes, so full of yearning that they looked dark. "My sweet Frankie," he sighed before lowering his face, nibbling gently on my lip. He pressed me closer before finally kissing me. His warm lips thawed the frozen feelings that I had packed away years ago and I knew I was in trouble.

Chapter 27
Ava

"Good morning!" I said cheerily as I floated down the white marble hallway of Closter Enterprises. I stopped at Gina's desk, placing a large floral bouquet on the center of her desk.

"What are these beauties for?" She asked, admiring the mix of hydrangeas and roses.

"Aren't they gorgeous!" I said excitedly. "I picked them up at the farmer's market. They are a gesture of gratitude for watching the kids last night. I really do appreciate it."

Gina swatted me with her hand, "Don't be silly, you make it sound like I took them for a week! It was four hours, Ava!"

"I know," I said, taking a seat on the edge of her desk. I bent down, inhaling the fresh scent of the roses. "They were four glorious hours."

"Glorious? Hmm, someone is glowing today. Let it out, I need the details."

"It was perfect, Gina!" I beamed with delight. "He picked me up in a red Vespa, just like the one he had when we were kids. We rode down to the marina and enjoyed sandwiches and seltzers."

"Sounds simple and relaxing. I don't think I've ever seen you this enthusiastic. Does this mean you finally had sex?" she asked with a wink.

"Gina! No!"

"Why not?" she asked, sounding disappointed.

"Gina, he's my boss."

"Liam was too and you considered that, didn't you?"

"No, I did not," I said, aggravated with her assumption. "And that is different. Nick is the CEO. Besides, we are just friends."

"Just friends?"

"Maybe we kissed," I confessed meekly.

"I knew it! What else?"

"That's all. Really, I'm not hiding anything. We talked, a lot, just like when we were kids. It was divine."

"Glorious. Divine. You sound in love!"

"No, nothing like that. As soon as the Laurents' sign the deal, this little arrangement of ours will be over and I'll go back to being Ava Agostini, assistant extraordinaire to Mr. Nicholas Closter, CEO."

"Right, about that, I'm not so sure everything is all roses between Liam and Samantha."

"What makes you think that?" I asked.

"I think Liam slept in his office last night."

"Really?" I asked. I don't know why but I had an empty, hollow feeling I couldn't explain over the realization that perhaps the arrangement with Nick would be over sooner than I thought. It left me sad.

I wasn't given much time to wallow, as the quick staccato of stilettos sounded from down the hall, coming from the direction of Nicholas' office. Gina and I both looked up to find the beautiful blond specimen, better known as Samantha Laurent, cat walking down the hallway, wearing a curve hugging blue dress that stopped at her knees.

She was reapplying her lipstick and fixing her hair, finally stopping at the elevator. She must have felt Gina's and my gaze upon her, as she swiftly turned to look at us. She flipped her blond hair over her shoulder and greeted us with a fake smile.

"Bonjour," she said.

"Hi," managed Gina flatly. Me, I only managed a feeble, apathetic wave.

The elevator dinged its arrival and Samantha Laurent disappeared into the elevator just as quickly as she had appeared. Her presence was brief but left me with lasting effects. Gina cleared her throat.

"Well, that was interesting," she said.

"Uh, yeah. That was Samantha Laurent, correct?" I asked.

"Yep."

"And she was coming out of Nicholas' office."

"We don't know that," contended Gina.

"Where else then? The conference rooms. Nothing else is down that hallway. She certainly didn't come out of her fiancé's office."

"No, that she did not."

"That conversation we were just having. Everything I just shared with you; forget it. Forget it all," I said.

"Oh Ava, stop, stop jumping to conclusions and shutting yourself off again."

"Whatever. I need to get to work. See you at lunch?"

"Yep, I'm getting pizza today, hope you like pineapple," she said with a radiant smile.

"Pineapple? On pizza? Seriously, Gina?" She nodded. "No! It's a hard no for me. Please, no pineapple on mine." I waved goodbye and turned to walk to my desk.

I don't know what I wanted to do or how I expected to act today but any thoughts of how I should act were clouded by the new vision of Samantha Laurent leaving Nick's office. It shouldn't bother me or get under my skin. I don't have the right to let it bother me. Only it did and that was a problem.

I placed my bag in the bottom drawer of my desk and set out for the break room to make Nick's coffee. My mind was mush as I watched the black coffee drip out of the machine.

I mechanically pulled two biscotti out from the glass jar and set them on the saucer before heading back to his office. I took a deep breath as I approached and what I heard next broke my heart for reasons I couldn't quite grasp.

"I see Samantha paid you a visit today? So, it worked?" I heard Luke say from inside Nick's open office.

"Yes, yes! It certainly did and in due time," replied Nick happily.

"Looks like everything turned out just the way you wanted them too. You might end up with the girl and the deal."

"Appears so. This is better than I could have hoped for."

"Congratulations, man!" exclaimed Luke.

"Thanks. Its congratulations for us all. Now we just have to get the contract signed quickly. I will be returning to Paris by the end of the month."

My heart sank. He got the girl and the deal. So, he was back with Samantha? And returning to Paris?

Chapter 28
Nicholas

Ava and I had a decent week together but oddly, we both didn't speak of the kiss or our time at the marina. I couldn't make heads or tails of the situation. She was a puzzle I couldn't figure out. We both clearly enjoyed each other's company and I felt in every fiber of my being that we both felt on fire for each other but this week at work it was odd, almost like our time together hadn't happened.

We had an unspoken need to not make things uncomfortable at work. I suppose that was it. We had come to an undeclared understanding and it was beneficial. It was ok, I suppose. I had to make it ok. We respected each other. I respected her too much to make it awkward. So, we joked, we laughed, we got things done. We worked well together but I longed to reconnect with her and she felt so distant.

She was the best assistant I ever had and she made my life easier. It was work as usual but I missed her. I missed the Ava I had a glimpse of when we had been together at the marina.

Initially, Ava and I had plans to attend Christopher and Alana's wedding together. That was before rumors started of Liam and Samantha's relationship being on the rocks. That was before Liam started coming to work intoxicated and sleeping in his office.

That was before Samantha paid me a visit at the office to tell me she was no longer engaged to my brother, begging me to take her back.

I don't know what changed, but shortly after Ava had a change of heart. She wedged distance between us once more and I no longer felt the same reception from her as she had shown at the marina. Now, Ava felt we no longer needed to carry on the charade, as she called it. Only to me it wasn't a charade and I wanted nothing more than to be at this wedding with her.

That was difficult enough to accept, but unbearable was the thought of never kissing her again, which left me hollow. That wasn't something I wanted but I needed to keep her in my life in whatever capacity possible, as I could no longer fathom a life without her in it. She wasn't ready for us to be anything more and maybe I wasn't either.

As far as business, the next few weeks would be busy and critical. I was due back in France by the end of the month to patch together the Laurent deal. I hoped the fiasco engagement between Liam and Samantha didn't burn bridges with the Laurents.

It was a breezy Saturday evening as I drove alone to Chris and Alanna's beach wedding. Alone. I was back to alone. I realized I have always been alone, never truly feeling not alone except when I was in Ava's presence. All the women throughout all the years, but they never filled the void. Only Ava ever had and only Ava ever would.

All of Vilamor was festively dressed in lights, ribbons and displays as we welcomed the most joyful time of the year but it wasn't joyful for me. Not anymore.

I was pretty miserable by the time I arrived, and as the evening went on I became increasingly disgruntled. I spent most of the night avoiding Liam and trying not to get noticed for staring at Ava every opportunity I could get. Yes, I was becoming that infatuated type that I hated all my life.

I stood at the edge of the dance floor, near the bar, because let's be honest, the bar was my friend tonight. I didn't arrive with intentions of drinking but not being with Ava while surrounded by loving couples made it painful to exist.

"Scotch, on the rocks please," I ordered to the bartender while placing a few bills in the glass tip jar.

"Ava's a sweet girl. I like her." I turned to see my aunt Debra had joined me.

"She is," I agreed. "How long have you been standing there?" I asked as she stepped closer.

"Long enough to see how you have been watching her."

"Is it that obvious?"

"Yes. If I didn't know better, I would suggest you love her."

"You think?" I smirked at her observation, while nodding my appreciation to the bartender as he handed me my drink. "Nah, not in this lifetime, Auntie."

"I don't think Niko, I know."

"Bringing out the old nickname? Only you and Mom called me that."

"Yes, maybe you'll listen better if I speak to you like a child." She clasped her hand around mine. "You love her. I see it in the way you look at her."

I shook my head, downing the scotch and waving to the bartender for another. My aunt always did have a 'third eye'; like a witch, she saw things no one else could.

"She softens you, Niko," she continued.

"We are very different people, Auntie." My eyes sought north until they laid sight upon Ava. My chest tightened. "We have different lives and different expectations," I mumbled more to myself than to my aunt as I watched Ava.

"Is that what you are worried about?" My aunt squeezed my hand. "Life's expectations? You mean the expectations of a Closter? Those imposed on you by your father." My aunt took a long-drawn-out sigh. "Your father has hardened over the years. I understand, losing a wife, the love of your life, so early can do that to a person but don't let that be you."

"I often think how things would have been if Mom was still here."

"We all do. Maybe you wouldn't have spent your adult life working so hard and running from love. Niko, I am proud of you."

"Yeah?" I questioned. Needing to hear her affirmation.

"Yes! I am very proud of you and I know your mother would be too. I know she'd be proud of you. But she also wouldn't want you wasting your life and ending up alone." She pointed toward Ava. "Your mom would like Ava."

"Ava's my assistant and—"

"And maybe you need to let her know how you feel. How you really feel," she replied, cutting me off.

"I don't know how to do that. Not without ruining things," I rubbed my chin in torment. "I've lost her once before; I can't lose her again."

"I know. Luke told me your story. Seems to me that God is giving you a second chance. Don't waste it. There may not be a third."

"Did Luke also tell you that Ava isn't in love with me? Did he tell you everything she did was for Liam?"

"How do you know that unless you ask her? Have you told her how you feel?" I nodded as she patted my arm. She leaned in closer. "I paid the DJ to play some oldies. You know your uncle won't get up to dance unless his beloved oldies are playing." She rolled her eyes. "Drives me nuts but it's my only chance to get a dance with him." We both laughed. "Why don't you go dance with her?"

I turned around to face the dance floor. My eyes quickly found Ava again. "She's having fun with Luke. Let her be."

"Luke needs to tend to his wife instead of zipping around the dance floor like a boy on spring break. Look at him!" she said as she rolled her eyes again. "Go, get in there." She took my drink and pushed me along.

I strolled onto the dance floor until I stood directly behind Ava. I remained behind her like a revering bodyguard.

"Luke!" screamed my aunt over the music.

"What, ma?" He replied, annoyed.

"Go get your wife a water and let Ava catch a breather."

My aunt gave him the devil eyes and pointed my direction. Luke followed her body language, finally noticing me standing behind Ava.

"Oh, hey Nick!" He waved enthusiastically. "Ava, sorry but maybe you and Nick can finish?"

I didn't dance to this stuff. Whatever this was that was playing. I hadn't since college and I would need a lot more liquid courage to bring back those moves.

Luke flung Ava around. She was flushed from the dancing and caught off guard at seeing me standing so close. She stumbled straight into my arms with the force of Luke's abrupt swing.

"Hey, I got you," I said, catching her.

She giggled like a schoolgirl. The music slowed down as the instrumental melody of a new song started playing. Perfect timing, something I could actually dance too. I held out my hands.

"May I?" I asked.

"Sure." She giggled.

We danced in the moonlight as an old classic piped through the speakers. I laughed to myself as I recognized the tune immediately. I glanced over to my aunt, who held her thumbs up.

"This is a great song." Ava started humming.

"It is." I shook my head in agreement. I sang along with the song as she hummed. She smiled and I felt her body relax into mine. Her chin laid on my shoulder and I turned my head, nuzzling my nose in her sweet-smelling hair. God, how I missed her scent and the feel of her in my arms. It had only been a week since I held her, but it was a week too long. I rested my chin on her head and took her in as she surrounded me.

We fit; I couldn't explain it better than to say that we fit. Like the missing puzzle piece that I had been searching for all my life. Here it was, my missing puzzle piece. This moment was perfect; the music, the breeze, the moonlight. She was perfect for me. An overwhelming feeling of being at peace with myself, with her, with the universe filled me and in that moment the world stopped. This was the kind of flawless night you get once in a lifetime.

It was too perfect. I became aware of movement and commotion coming from the edge of the dance floor. I turned to see Luke holding Liam by the arm before Liam dashed toward me.

"Sorry cuz, I tried!" Explained Luke.

Ava stopped dancing and turned at the sound of Luke's voice.

"Ava, let's dance," suggested Liam.

"Hi, Liam," she said flatly.

Another day, another drunk Liam, was I surprised? No, not at all.

"I'm dancing with your brother but maybe after."

People were starting to watch; they were taking notice. I caught my aunt's worried look. I didn't want to spoil the night and I knew Liam's current state of mind. The perfect moment was over.

"It's fine," I said, releasing Ava. "There will be other dances." I put distance between us, seeing the fleeting look of disappointment in Ava's eyes but she didn't object as I walked back toward the bar.

I stood there, only briefly. I was done with it all. Done with this whole scene before I even arrived. How many lovesick happy couples could someone surround themselves with? I was encircled by love at every corner. Sure, it was a wedding and it was to be expected but this was more than I could stomach.

It was everywhere I looked. I had enough by the time my eyes settled back on Liam dancing with Ava. I didn't want to watch. I couldn't watch them. It made me sick, physically sick.

I started walking. I left the bar, left the dance floor and left the party far behind me. My legs carried me and I kept walking through the cool sand along the surf. I distanced myself from all of it and all the people. I walked and walked and kept walking until I was far away enough to not hear the laughing, the chatting and the music.

When I was far enough away, I bent down, taking a seat on the sand and looked out over the surf that gleamed white in the moonlight. I don't know how long I sat by myself and I don't know how long she had been following me but I knew Ava was there before she even spoke. It was some bizarre sixth sense I had developed.

"A penny for your thoughts," her voice whispered to me. I felt the smile creep upon my face when she spoke. That was the great thing about her, she always could pull me out of my moods. It was an enigma; she made me ill but just as quickly healed me. Ava was both my illness and my remedy.

"Are my thoughts that cheap?" I responded.

"Depends on who is paying," she said with a smile.

"I suppose." I played with the sand, letting it sift through my fingers. "Is that how much they are worth to you, Ava?"

"No." Her voice lowered to an almost inaudible whisper. "They are worth much more." She shifted her weight from foot to foot. "May I join you?"

I gestured to my left. She lifted her dress and lowered herself to the sand, sitting close enough that her body heat warmed me. We sat in silence and it was perfect.

"Déjà vu," she said.

"Yeah." I thought about this beach, and our sitting here together all those years ago. "I would say so."

"Sitting at the edge here, enjoying the sound of the waves in good company."

"Sounds right. You, me and this beach. Those were the best days," I added.

I allowed myself to finally look her way. I fought it long enough and I knew it could be a mistake. It was becoming increasingly more difficult to be around her. Almost painful, but God, she was a sight for my eyes. She was ethereal. She looked lovely in the moonlight, smiling coyly at me and I saw the faint blush that crept upon her cheeks.

She turned her gaze away from me and looked back out to the sea but I remained looking at her. It was a beautiful night with the full moon and I registered that moment in my mental catalog, not wanting to forget how she looked and how this moment felt.

She raised her champagne glass to her lips and I observed the white strap of her dress as it slipped down her shoulder. She was unaware and the strap remained there in that manner. I yearned to touch her. Fighting the internal demons, I finally allowed my index finger to run the length of her upper arm, as I lifted the strap back to its rightful place at the top of her shoulder.

She turned her gaze to watch my finger. I let it linger there, as I rubbed soft circles on her shoulder committing the feel of her skin to memory. I leaned down, brushing my lips on her shoulder as I looked up to meet her eyes.

I was pushing the envelope and taking risks. I took a deep breath, I let my forehead lay on her shoulder for a few seconds longer as I inhaled her sweet scent. I just wanted the moment to last a little longer. I wanted the feeling, the stillness and the fragrance, all of it to sear my brain so that I would never forget it. I wanted to have this memory forever, to be able to access it until the day I was old, gray and dying.

I felt her tremble and tense. God, how I wish I could read her mind, even once, briefly enough to look into the corners of her mind. I wanted to know what she thought and how she felt. What made her heart race? She was guarded with impenetrable walls and I wanted to tear them all down.

I felt a lump form in my chest. I spoke senselessly without thought, "do you believe that love transcends time and space?" I don't know why I asked that question. Or what that really even meant. What kind of question was that to ask? It felt ridiculous as it escaped my lips.

"What?" She sounded confused. "I'm not really sure what you are asking."

"Oh, Ava!" I lifted my head from her shoulder and rubbed my hands down my face, anguished with longing and wanting. I shook my head, needing to say it but knowing I shouldn't. I answered my own question, "it does Ava, it really does."

She stared at me intently. "Don't say anymore, Nick."

Her words were a sucker punch to my heart. It wasn't what I wanted to hear but I obeyed her wishes. We sat in silence for a few minutes. Both of us watching the waves and quietly living in our heads. Then she spoke and I wished she hadn't.

"I don't know how to say this but I know it needs to be said." She took a deep breath and when I looked at her, I saw that her eyes were glassy. "Sometimes in life, there are these really special moments. The kind that looking back you go 'whoa that was big, that was important', right? But life is all about experiences and decisions and we take actions that lead us down certain paths and once you take those paths, you can't go back or shouldn't go back."

"What are you saying, Ava? I'm not following."

"We had a moment, Nick. We can't deny it. We had more than a moment. We had a whole summer of moments and experiences and memories. Maybe it was meant to have been more but we made our choices then and life has moved on. That moment is gone, Nick. It is a part of our past where it belongs."

She leaned over, closer, and I yearned to touch her. I wanted to put my arms around her. Her lips brushed against my cheek with an innocent kiss that lit me up. She branded me forever hers even if she didn't want me. She pulled away and I was filled with anguish. "Leave it where it belongs, Nick. Please, just leave it."

She quickly stood up and jogged back to the party and I allowed my eyes to follow her silhouette until it disappeared, engulfed by the darkness.

Chapter 29
Ava

I left Nick as quickly as I could; picking up my pace the further I got so I wouldn't change my mind and return. I needed to escape, escape his burning gaze and leave before he said something that neither of us could take back.

Dear God, he was close to admitting his feelings and I couldn't allow that. It was better for everyone, especially him and me if we just left things as they were. Leave it in the past, before we got to the point of no return.

I didn't admit to him or myself that I recognized him that first day at the café. How could I not recognize him? How could I not recognize the familiar feeling of his arms around me? The truth was I didn't let him say it all those years ago and I couldn't allow him to say it now.

August 2000-Vilamor

I packed the last of my toiletries into my suitcase and sat at the edge of my bed, searching in my purse for my passport. The day had come. The end of August and I was days away from returning to school. I heard the shuffling footstep of my grandmother coming down the long Spanish tiled hallway.

"Francesca!" She snapped.

"Sim avozinha (Yes, grandma)," I answered my grandmother in our native knowing how much she appreciated it.

"Esta aqui um rapaz a tua procura (There is a young man looking for you), she said, folding her hands together."

"Esta a minha procura? (Looking for me?)"

"Sim diz que se chama Nicholas. (Yes, he says his name is Nicholas.)"

Oh crap! Nick? What is he doing here? I jogged out of my room, down the long hallway in search of him, finding him outside standing near his Vespa in the shade of an olive tree. He was wearing navy blue swimming trunks and had a white beach towel draped around his neck. His skin was tan and glistened from the suntan lotion and salty ocean water.

"Trying to get me in trouble, are you?" I jested.

His face broke out with a smirk. "She's a tough one!" He responded, regarding my grandmother. "She wasn't too pleased to see me."

"No, of course not, you are a boy and I'm her only granddaughter," I said as if that explained it all. Maybe it did, maybe it didn't.

"Enough said," he laughed.

I watched him. I watched his jittery gestures and his unusual stance. I waited for him to say whatever it was he came here to say. We looked at each other far longer than we should have. I glanced over my shoulder to see if grandma was there. Luckily, she was not. Nick shuffled his weight from one leg to the other and cleared his throat.

"The time was going by and it was just habit to come see you," he started, "I know you are leaving soon for the airport but I wanted to tell you that this summer has been a pleasant surprise." He looked away from me, his hands holding tightly to the ends of the towel that was arranged around his shoulders. I watched as he bit his lower lip in thought.

"A pleasant surprise," he continued, "One I hadn't expected this early in my life." He looked back my way. His eyes traveled over me, finally settling on my eyes where I liked them so I could feel the warmth of his large, brown eyes. He took a few steps toward me, his breathing was rapid. "I don't know if I am ready but I can't let you leave without telling you that I lo—"

"I'll be back next summer," I said, cutting him off. I cut him off as quickly as I could. I knew what he was about to say, I was young but not naïve and nope, I wasn't going to let him say it. I took a few steps back to put more distance between us.

"I can't wait for next summer," he added. "I can't go a year without talking to you. A year without hearing your voice. How can I contact you? How can I reach you?"

"I am going back to New York to finish school and you'll be away in college."

"Yes, but—"

"But nothing, Nick. We will see each other in Vilamor, again. In a year. I come to Vilamor every summer. We will catch up then. Maybe more Vespa

rides, seaside strolls and ice creams." I smiled at him, holding back the tears that pooled at the back of my eyes.

"And if you don't come back or I don't? What if we don't cross paths?" He asked.

"Do you believe in fate? In divine intervention. Do you believe that things are just meant to be?" His eyes furrowed at my questions. "I do," answering for the both of us. "If we are meant to meet again, the universe will make it happen. We will collide once more, in due time."

"You are leaving this up to the universe?" His eyes narrowed.

"Yes, just like it put us in each other's path that day I hung from the cliff." I smiled at the memory. "Thank you for coming, Nick. This was a nice surprise."

I walked closer to him and wrapped my arms around his neck, hugging him in what I hoped would not be the last. He hugged me back too. It was a hug we both needed. I laid my weight on him and he laid his on me and we supported each other. He ran his hand down my hair, smoothing it and laid his lips to the top of my head, dusting it with a soft kiss.

"Ok. Until next year," he said.

"Yep, you know where to find me," I answered.

That was twenty-two years ago. Sure, it was much later in life than either one of us planned but the universe did in fact bring us back together. We quite literally collided but now what? Where do we go from here? In theory, it is all happening as we had once hoped but with obstacles in the way.

I am an exhausted mother to two children; he an executive who doesn't want children. We aren't the sunset chasing teenagers with no ties and our whole futures ahead of us.

I continued with my pondering mind, treading through the cool sand, returning to the party. A party I wish I had come to with him. The beach was now flecked with multiple fire pits surrounded by wedding guests enjoying late night treats. Gina was one of them. Her smile widened as she saw me coming and wobbled toward me with a smore in hand.

"Hey, what's going on?" she said giddily. "I am having such a good time but I've been looking for you," she said, out of breath.

"I went for a walk."

"Here," she said, handing me a smore. "They are delish. I'm going to the bar to get a drink, want to come with?"

"Sure."

We walked arm in arm barefooted until we reached the wraparound bar.

"Gosh, this smore is good! I haven't had a smore in ages," I said.

"I know! I am salivating just thinking about the next one I am going to devour." We both laughed.

"Well, well, what do we have here? What are my ex-assistant and my current assistant up to?"

The hairs rose on the back of my neck as the familiar voice sounded inches from me. I felt the weight of Liam's upper body as he rested his arm on my shoulder. His words were slurred and the stench of liquor draped between us. He had clearly dedicated his time tonight to drinking and perhaps little else.

"Just hydrating so we can get back to the fire pits for another smore. Maybe you'd like to hydrate too," suggested Gina.

"I do want to hydrate. Maybe you can spare Ava. I need a drinking partner and a dancing partner."

"What can I get you ladies?" asked the bartender.

"I'll have a seltzer with lime," responded Gina.

The bartender nodded and turned his attention to me. "And you, miss?"

"She'll have a scotch on the rocks," answered Liam on my behalf, "make it two, I'll have one also."

"Just make it one, please," I held up my finger to the bartender. "I'll stick with a seltzer lime as well."

"Oh, come on Ava, live a little. Have some fun with me," teased Liam.

I moved my eyes to Gina, avoiding Liam, he didn't need the attention.

"Shouldn't your fiancé fill the roles of both dance partner and drinking partner?" asked Gina.

"My fiancé?" he asked, puzzled. "She's gone. Yep, she left."

"I'm sorry to hear that, Liam," sympathized Gina, although everyone had already speculated.

"Yeah, whatever. Win some, lose some," he justified. "I would rather talk about the present than the past," he said, moving my hair over my shoulder.

"Gina," he continued, "did you know that Ava has refused to drink with me all evening. Rather boring, isn't she? I don't understand it, she has had no qualms drinking with my brother but can't be bothered with me." I shifted my weight, adding distance between us although he made it impossible.

"She didn't even know who my brother was a couple months ago and now they are inseparable." He moved to face me and held my chin, lifting my face toward him, "and I've been shut out."

The bartender certainly was taking his sweet time. Did seltzer with lime require any preparation? I was uncomfortable and moved to leave.

"Hey!" he said with a deep, sterner voice than I had ever heard from him. He commanded the attention of not just me but all those around us. "Where are you going?"

"You know, on second thought, I've lost my thirst. I think I'll head back for a smore."

He gripped my wrist, tightening his hold on me and I knew then that this was going to turn ugly.

***

Nicholas

I headed back to the party. I had moped enough and the self-reflection was becoming depressing. As I approached, the view was lit with fire pits illuminating the shore. My intentions, as I walked back, were to grab a cigar, take a smoke, hang out for another hour and find Ava to continue the conversation we were having. Hopefully, I would leave with her.

I walked leisurely, taking my time. I thought about what I wanted to say to her and how I would say it. I didn't want to assail her; no, I wanted her to be at ease. I was living in my head, unaware of Luke jogging toward me.

"Your brother's a mess!" He shouted.

"And?" I asked, continuing my leisurely walk with my hands comfortably in my pockets.

"And he is becoming a distraction," he added, out of breath.

"Tell him to go home."

"I was hoping you could do that or talk to your dad about it."

"My dad? Seriously? Liam isn't a kid. Besides, he's the golden child. You honestly think my father would send him home?"

Luke kept pace with me as we walked back. He didn't reply and I knew what his silence meant. He wanted me to fix it. "Where is he?" I asked.

Luke moved his hand, spilling beer in the process as he directed my attention to the bar. "Over there. I don't like how close he is to Gina. He is a mess. One slip and he takes Gina down with him."

My eyes searched and then I saw him. What an ass he was. His partially unbuttoned shirt was untucked, his tie loosened around his neck looking like the complete disheveled mess that he had become. But it wasn't how he personally looked that made my chest tighten and burn, it was the site of his arm leaning on Ava that perturbed me.

"Just go cut him off!" I exclaimed, aggravated by the situation.

"Well, I don't want to be rude."

"Rude? You are worried about being rude? I don't understand you; for weeks, you annoyed me about not making a scene at the engagement party or the wedding and here is my brother doing exactly that and you are worried about being rude or offending him. Why does everyone give him passes in life? I'm done with this shit." I advanced toward the bartender.

I respected Luke, Christopher and my aunt enough to not make a scene. I quietly approached the opposite end of the bar and motioned for the bartender.

"That gentleman over there," I said, pointing to Liam. "Has he ordered any alcoholic beverages?"

"Yes, he just ordered a scotch on the rocks."

"Ok, listen to me, he is cut off. Do not serve him anymore." I passed over a $100 bill. "Understood?" The bartender nodded, taking the money.

***

Ava

"Where are you going in such a hurry?" Liam spewed at me. "I have seen you drink and dance and laugh with my brother for weeks now and damn it, Ava, you are going to do it with me too."

"Liam, you're drunk. You've had too much to drink and I am going home," I said.

"I am drunk," he agreed, "but you're not going anywhere."

"Yes, I am." I stood up to leave. "I have been humiliated and continue to be with your sloppy behavior. This isn't fun anymore."

"Get back here." He grabbed my wrist and turned me around.

"Liam, let go of my wrist, you're hurting me." He pulled me nearer and I was now stuck between the cold, hard unmoving edge of the bar and an equally unmoving Liam. His breath smelled of the hard liquor he had been drinking. He reeked of it. It saddened me as he never used to drink.

"Everything out of your mouth is a complaint or a no. Is that how you were with my brother?"

"No," I said.

"No? Why not?"

"No because your brother, unlike you, is a gentleman. He can hold his liquor."

"Amusing of you to remind me. That is exactly what Samantha said to me before she left."

"What's gotten into you? Is that why you've been drinking? Because she left?"

"She left, yes but no, I don't care about her. I'm not drinking because of her." He walked around me to get closer to where the bartender stood.

"Bartender! Over here. Where's my drink? And a double for the lady too."

"I don't want anything; I don't want to drink."

"Yes, you do. She'll have a double. Maybe that will loosen you up." He frustratingly undid his tie, pulling it off. "I've spent the past year trying to get you to see me as more than your boss and you never did and my brother strolls back in town and he's got you salivating at his feet. He got the best of you. Didn't he? When do I get the best of you?"

"I have orders to cut you off, sir," said the bartender.

"Orders to cut me off? Orders from who? You get those drinks and you get them now." He had the bartender by the collar. I grabbed his arm.

"Liam, what's gotten into you? Let him go," I pleaded.

"Don't tell me what to do Ava, don't ever tell me what to do!" He flung me back into the stool so violently that I missed and fell on the floor.

"Liam, what the hell?" Questioned Gina as she bent down to help me up. "Ava, are you ok?" Her pregnant frame blocked the view but I heard it. I heard the distinct sound of a fist hitting a jaw.

Gina turned at the sound as a swarm of people gathered. The funny thing about a bar fight was how quickly people gathered to witness the fight like bees on honey. When I was back on my two feet, I allowed my eyes to take in the view.

Liam was laying on the sand with Luke and Christopher hovering over him, helping him to stand back up. Not far off was Nick shaking out his arm, cursing.

"I warned you Liam, I told you to never put your hands on her again. You're a mess. Go home." Nick turned around and that's when I saw his red hand and Liam's bloodied lip.

Mrs. Closter approached the scene, crying and Mr. Closter was not far behind, consoling his wife and rambling on about Liam drinking too much. I couldn't believe this was all happening. It all happened so quickly. I couldn't believe that two brothers had gotten physical but it was obviously bound to happen.

"What the hell is going on?" I sadly asked Gina.

"Oh, lord help us. Very clearly looks like Nick swung at Liam."

I shook my head in disbelief as I took steps backward, wanting to distance myself.

"You!" Shouted Kate Closter, pointing at me. "It's your fault! You whore!" She walked toward me faster than I could react. The venom was dripping from her voice. She stood inches from me.

"You bounced from Liam to Nick. This is your fault. And why? So you could gain yourself money and a new prestigious last name." I couldn't even stop her or brace myself as her right hand raised up and connected with my cheek in a slap that rang out in my ears. Anyone who hadn't been watching the scene before, certainly was now. "Leave my family alone!"

"Kate!" Nick grabbed Kate around the waist and carried her away from me. I stood, embarrassed and dazed. "Dad, take your drunk wife home. Do something right for once in your life. Do something for me once in your life."

"What is that supposed to mean?" asked Mr. Closter.

"Exactly what it sounds like. Go!" He ordered. "Take her home."

My face burned with a stinging, vibrating sensation that took over the whole left side of my face. I raised my hand to my cheek to find it was numb and swelling.

"Let's get you some ice, Ava," Gina said, ushering me back toward the bar.

"I'll be fine." I wanted the attention off me. I didn't want to make this any bigger than it already was.

"Sure, you will be fine but the ice will help. Come on."

The DJ announced the cutting of the cake. Perfect timing! Yes, the best thing to do to get the evening back on track. As we approached the bar, we were met by Nick, who was there holding a white linen napkin twisted with ice inside.

"I got it, Gina," he reassured her. "Go ahead, relax yourself, rest your feet and get some cake. Luke is worried about you." He patted Gina on the shoulder.

Gina smiled. "Will you be alright?" She asked me. "I think I am leaving you in good hands."

"Yes, definitely," I nodded. "I'm fine, go ahead."

I watched as she left, wishing I could crawl under the bar and disappear but obviously that wasn't going to happen. I looked back at Nick with sad eyes. What a night full of every emotion. His gaze was still on me. I couldn't read his eyes but I knew they were saying so much. He stood adjacent and his presence overwhelmed me.

"Looks like you need ice yourself," I pointed to his roughened hand.

"I feel fine. I think I am too drunk to feel any pain," he rubbed his knuckles but I felt he meant more than the physical pain.

"Have a seat," he said and I did as he directed, sliding onto the smooth acrylic barstool.

"That was a nasty slap," he nodded while twisting the ice in the napkin. He held my chin similarly to how Liam had but Nick's grip was gentle, kind and welcomed.

"Does it look as bad as it feels?" I asked, squinting upon his placement of the ice on my cheek.

He tilted his head, examining my face. "I won't lie, it is swelling up faster than I would have expected." I observed his actions toward me and his overly concerned manner. I took in the feel of his thumb as it rubbed over my cheek and I watched his eyes while they appraised my injury. He cared, he genuinely seemed to care.

"Twice in two weeks, I find you tending to my wounds."

He arched his eyebrows and nodded in agreement. "Both wounds are inadvertently my fault. It is the least I can do."

"This wasn't your fault, Nick." I covered his hand with mine. "Don't put the blame on yourself."

"Why don't you go home, Liam? I think it is time," Luke's voice spoke from behind us, startling me. I turned to see Liam plop on a bar stool. I turned back to Nick, taking my hand up to his that held the ice at my cheek. I took the ice from him.

"I got it. Thank you," I said.

He sighed and dropped his hand.

"Ok." He shook his head, understanding the unspoken meaning behind my statement. "I think I should leave before any other scenes are made. I'll head home," he said.

"That is a great idea. Drive safe, brother," waved Liam cynically.

Nick hugged me, squeezing me harder than he ever had. It felt good. He leaned closer, whispering in my ear, "Please call me if he becomes too much to handle, ok?"

I nodded and then pulling away, looked at him with appreciative eyes.

Liam tugged on Nick's jacket sleeves, "Ok, ok, that's enough. Go on now."

"Good night." Nick turned and left, leaving me alone with Liam. I watched him, wishing I could enjoy his company more and knowing that wouldn't be wise. But I did know what would be wise.

"Come on Liam, let's go home," I said. "I'll drive."

Gina grabbed my arm and it stopped me with a jolt. I didn't want to look at her, I didn't want her to see what I was thinking or worse yet what I was feeling. When I looked back at her, my eyes were met with her confused ones.

"Ava, what are you doing?" She asked.

"I am going home."

"With Liam?" She questioned.

"Yes. No worries. He's not driving. He's had so much to drink that he will pass out once he gets in the car." We both looked at Liam as he swayed, holding himself up against the edge of the bar counter.

"That's not what I mean," she held both my hands in hers. "You are going home with the wrong brother, Ava." Her voice was pleading. She wasn't saying the words but I knew she was begging me to go with Nicholas.

I shook my head, "No, I'm not, Gina. Aren't you the one that always pushed me toward Liam?"

"That was months ago. That was before Nick came into your life. Don't do this, Ava. Don't go home with Liam, you're going to regret it tomorrow."

"No Gina, that's where you're wrong. I'll regret it if I go home with Nick. This is how it is supposed to be." I placed my hand over hers, reassuring her but also to release her grip on my arm. "No worries, Gina. Please. Enjoy your night."

Chapter 30
Nicholas

I lugged the glass tumbler toward my lips and winced at the tingling pain that radiated across my knuckles. What happened tonight? How quickly everything had gotten so ugly.

My intentions hours before when I was returning to the party was in setting out to finally tell Ava how I felt, whether she wanted to hear it or not. I was going to take my aunt's advice and tell her everything. That was short lived once I saw Liam and Ava.

It was a knock to the head to see him so close to her. The visual of Liam touching her and shoving her made me see red. I swung at him before I could even process my actions.

But the worst, the part of the evening that had my chest hurting and my brain numb, was seeing Ava go home with him. Never did I think she would leave with him. I guess I naively thought there was something between us but what I thought we had, she so clearly had for Liam, not me.

So now, here I was at half past midnight, sitting in the air-conditioned lounge area with my ass planted on a cushy white leather bar stool with my only companion being the scotch on the rocks and the bartender who served me.

"Wow!" exclaimed Luke as he plopped down on a seat next to me. "I think you've had enough to drink, cousin."

The truth? I didn't plan on permanently planting myself at the bar. I came in here because I wanted to keep an eye on Ava, make sure my brother didn't get too handsy with her. But that all changed after I saw them leave together. At that point, I just wanted to get numb. I was in an unforeseen pain.

"She's going to be the death of me," I pathetically admitted.

"Ok, come on! I think you are being a little dramatic. I think you are letting the liquor talk. You'll feel much better about all of this tomorrow after you sober up."

"No, really, she's killing me." I brought the tumbler to my lips again, letting the warmth of the amber liquid fill me.

"Slowly," I emphasized, "it's a slow death."

Am I really going to admit this out loud? I guess I might as well as the only way out of this pain was through it. "My chest hurts every time she comes around. I get this pressure, right here," I pointed to my chest and squeezed my fist.

"Have you told her this?" Luke asked.

"No, of course not!" I said, placing the tumbler down on the granite counter with a thud. "What am I supposed to say? Hey, I feel like I'm having a heart attack every time you come around."

Luke chuckled. "Maybe don't use those words."

"I need to clear my mind, Luke. I need to get away."

"Nick, I really think you've had enough to drink. I haven't seen you drink this much in, well, never. How about I take you home?"

"Nah, I'm not going home. I don't want to go home. Take me to the airport."

"What?"

"It was always Liam. That was who she wanted. That's why she agreed to this ridiculous deal. It was always to get him. I thought I loved her enough that I could make her love me back."

"You love her? You know this?" asked Luke.

I nodded.

"Tell her! You need to tell her. Now. Call her and tell her."

"She's happy," I lamented, "she got what she wanted or who she wanted. I don't want to ruin it for her." I ran my hand through my hair, pulling on the ends, hoping that pain would dull the pain in my heart.

"You've never been a quitter. Never! So now you're quitting?"

"It's not quitting, it's waking up."

"You're running away," Luke said, clutching at my sleeve to grab my full attention.

"Moving on," I clarified.

"Where are you going?"

"France."

"Back to Samantha, to console her post failed engagement?" he asked, shaking his head in disappointment.

"No. I need to salvage the Laurent deal. Business was always the only thing that has never failed me so I'm getting back to what I know." I drained my glass and slammed it on the counter. "Now, are you taking me to the airport or should I call for a ride?"

"Stay the rest of the weekend and then Monday, if you feel the same way, I will personally take you to the airport."

"What will it matter? What will that change?"

"Exactly, it won't matter whether you leave today, tomorrow, Monday but maybe things will change or you will feel differently."

I wouldn't feel differently. Luke didn't know what I felt. I felt heartache, for the first time and I didn't have experience with it. I was the one that went around breaking hearts, not the other way around. I couldn't deal with the pain. I didn't know how to deal with the pain. It didn't matter how many days I waited; this pain would always be there.

Chapter 31
Ava

I hardly slept and I stopped trying after I saw the first break of dawn. I tiptoed outside in my robe and remained there until it was a decent enough hour to start the day. The evening and weeks leading up to this mess ran over and over in my mind until I felt physically sick.

I was distressed and so very, very sad over how everything played out. A broken engagement, two brothers fighting, a shattered Closter family bond, a beautiful wedding tarnished with violence and me back to unfeeling and alone. I wanted to fix it all and was unsure of how to do that.

I made two strong coffees and walked my way toward my couch to where Liam still slept. I was thankful I took Mrs. Santos up on her offer to let the kids' sleepover. This would have been difficult to explain to a three and six-year-old. How would I explain why Mommy's boss was sleeping on our couch? Better yet, why his face was black and blue or why he smelled like a bar.

As I had predicted last night, Liam fell fast asleep as soon as he was in the car. We barely made it a block before I heard him snoring. I managed to wake him long enough to drag him into the house and onto my couch.

I sat on my coffee table and gently nudged him. He turned his face toward me, initially dazed and then smiled.

"Good morning," I said dryly.

"Good morning? Is it morning already? Shit." He rubbed his eyes with his palms before sitting up. "Damn, how much did I drink last night?"

"Does it matter? I feel like all you've done for weeks now is drink without pause." I handed him the cup of coffee. "Here, have this and then I'll make us some French toast. Maybe it will help soak up the liquor."

"Thanks," he said, taking the coffee from me. He winced with pain as he brought the coffee to his lips. "That hurts," he brought his hand to his lip. "I have bits and pieces of memories from last night but I am hoping they are all just parts of a nightmare."

"What do you remember?" I asked.

"Nick hit me? My mom hit you?"

"Ah, yeah, that sounds about right," I confirmed.

"Shit, my mom really hit you? What the hell!"

"She slapped me, yes, after she called me a whore."

"I'm so sorry, Ava. Shit, I'm really sorry."

"What's going on, Liam? What's been going on with you lately?"

"Samantha and I broke things off. She was nagging constantly. I didn't love her. She didn't love me. She still loves my brother or maybe she loves the idea of being Nicholas Closter's wife. And she was jealous of you."

"Jealous of me?" I questioned.

"Yeah, she was so jealous of you and Nick. She saw how you two were together. She saw how close you and Nick were getting and honestly, it made me jealous too. The final straw came when she saw how I was with you."

"Moment of truth Liam, why did you get engaged?"

He didn't hesitate, "To piss off my brother." He shook his head and rubbed his chin. "My mother thought it would help me look like the favorable one with the board and if I didn't succeed, then I could use Laurent to compete with Closter Enterprises."

"Only I wasn't banking on my feelings for you. I wasn't thinking about what really marrying Samantha meant. The more I saw you with Nick, the more I saw it as another win for Nick and another loss for me. Nick was always the go getter, the successful one and he was successfully winning you too."

"Wow!" I sighed as I took in the details. I stood up and paced my living room.

"It was fake, Liam," I admitted, "it was all fake. Nick and I aren't together, we've never been together. It was all to break you and Samantha up and to ensure the Laurent deal went through."

"I don't believe you," he said, taking a sip of his coffee.

"It's true."

"I see how my brother looks at you. I see how you look at him. You may have gone into it pretending but my brother loves you, Ava and I think you love him too."

"It doesn't matter," I said, pacing. "None of it matters."

"Don't say that. Don't make last night all for nothing."

"So now what?" I asked, unsure of the direction either one of us should take.

"I'm not sure," he drained his coffee. "This is all fresh but after last night, blacking out and the way my mom treated you. I think a new start away from my mother's influence is what I need."

"I think that is a good idea," I agreed.

"And for you?" He asked.

"I don't know."

Chapter 32
Ava

I staggered into Closter Enterprise the following morning. My anxiety couldn't take another day away. I longed to get back to work, out of the house and out of my mind. My whole being impatiently needed to see Nick. I feared that Saturday's events had ruined our relationship forever in all ways and I just needed to see him and know all was well.

"Good morning, George!" I waved in the direction of the security desk.

"Good morning, Ava," he replied with a wave.

I hastily pressed on the elevator keypad. The feeling that I couldn't get upstairs fast enough was having me consider using the stairs. The elevator dinged and the door slid open. I pounced into the elevator, fixing my hair and dress as I rode up to the 5th floor.

I stumbled out of the elevator in an anticipatory hurry. I headed for Nick's office but I was shocked to find it was empty. The lights were off and his computer was shut down with no sign of him. I left his office and headed to Gina's desk.

"You were in a hurry this morning. You didn't even stop here first to say hello. That's unlike you."

"Where is he, Gina?" I asked, unable to waste time with small talk.

"Which one?" she asked flatly.

"Nicholas. Where is Nicholas?"

"He is gone."

"Gone?" Such a simple word that packed so much meaning and pain.

"Yes. I told you that you would regret leaving with Liam."

"Where is he, Gina? Where did he go?" Fearing the answer and not wanting to hear it.

"To France."

My heart sunk. "He's in France?"

"Yes, he left Saturday night. He went straight to the airport from the wedding. Luke tried to convince him to stay until today but he wouldn't listen."

"What? Why?" I asked, bewildered.

"Seriously, Ava?" Gina sat back in her chair, throwing her pen onto her desk and folding her arms over her chest. "What did you think he would do? You left the wedding with his brother! The brother that mere moments before he laid hands on all out of respect and love for you. Are you registering the impact? He stood up for you and instead of thanking him and spending time with him, you left with his brother."

"Ok, enough! I chose to go home with Liam because I knew nothing would happen with him. But I couldn't say the same thing with regards to Nick. If I had gone home with Nick, I wouldn't be able to control the situation. I feared he and I would take it to the next level and it would have changed everything forever."

"And that would have been so bad? Looks to me as though everything already has changed."

"Maybe. I don't know. I do know that Nick's life and my life don't fit together. Liam was the safer choice. No opening up to one another. No trusting our hearts to one another. No relationship. No love. No marriage. No divorce. And no one gets hurt."

"You mean you don't get hurt? Aren't you already hurting?"

"I can't let him ruin me for good. I can't break again." I walked back toward the elevator. "I don't want to be here anymore."

"Where are you going?" Gina asked with furrowed brows.

"Home," I replied blandly.

"Home?"

"Yes, I am taking a sick day."

I drove home in a fog. My unconscious mind dragged me back to Saturday, bringing me so much heartache and my conscious mind tried desperately to shove those memories deep into the recesses of my mind. I was going into protect mode. I knew it all too well.

I changed into pajamas and went to bed. I stayed in bed all day until it was time to pick up the kids and then I did it all over again the next day. My heart was hurting and blaming my head for my actions and it was more than my body could handle so I slept it off.

Chapter 33
Nicholas
Paris

I was grateful I chose to leave Vilamor during the holidays. Sure, it was an abrupt and unplanned departure but I couldn't handle the holidays close to Ava but not with Ava. I couldn't handle being an observer to everyone else's holiday joys when I, myself, was wallowing in regret, resentment, loneliness and heartbreak.

Being in France allowed me the freedom to live ambiguously and not have to make decisions as far as my personal life. Here in France, it was just work and business. Exactly how my old self liked it. I spent three weeks sealing the Laurent deal and although I was no longer needed here, I couldn't find a reason to return to Vilamor anymore.

I sat at my old desk in the Parisian office, looking out the window at the bustling streets below. It was raining and I missed Vilamor's sunshine. My phone vibrated in my jacket pocket. I pulled it out and a deep sense of guilt filled me as I read Liam's name across the screen.

I swiped up to accept the call. "What's this I read about you transferring to Paris? Is it true?"

"Hey! Yeah, I'm taking that promotion you offered. What is the title? Chief Operating Officer?" He questioned.

"I thought you had a life in Vilamor and didn't want to move?"

He took an audible sigh before responding. "I think it is time for a change."

"This is just like you, baby brother," I frustratingly responded, tapping my pen on the desk. "You are the child who begged for the Christmas gift, plays with it once and then moves on."

"What are you talking about?"

"Are you bored with Ava already?" I asked. "You got her and now you're running away and moving on?"

"What do you mean I got her?" His voice sounded irritated.

"You won, right?" I added. "You got Ava. You went home with her after Chris' wedding."

"Is that what you think?" He chuckled. "Yeah, I wanted Ava. I thought I wanted Ava but she wouldn't have me."

His words seeped in as I registered their meaning. "Is that what you've been thinking?" He asked. "Yes, she took me home after Chris' wedding but nothing happened. I didn't lay a hand on her."

"What do you mean? Enlighten me," I said, trying hard to sound uninterested.

"I mean she took my drunk ass home to her house. I slept on her couch and she made me breakfast, dude."

I remained silent, letting his words settle. I was sure they had moved their relationship onto the next level, making me and her forever impossible.

"You didn't really think that Ava and I hooked up, did you?" Liam asked, breaking the uneasy silence. "You didn't really think that she and I were a thing, did you?"

"I don't know. I thought for sure all this time she was just trying to get with you."

"Nah. She doesn't want me, Nick. I won't say that I didn't want her, sure she's a great girl but I'm not the one she wants. Honestly, I care too much about her and respect you too much at this point. I think you and I have done enough to each other over the years and maybe it's time to bury that hatchet."

"Let's not get ahead of ourselves, baby brother."

He let out a chuckle. "Fair enough."

Silence sat between us. We didn't do this, we didn't talk. The sad truth was we didn't know how to be brothers. We had a strained relationship. We were detached, had been since birth. I was not saying I was not willing to try but we wouldn't become friends overnight.

"So, your old assistant Collette," Liam started.

"Yes, my old assistant Collette will be your new assistant."

"Right," he sighed, "is she single?"

"If you're asking me if she's married, the answer is no. She has been dating people. Last time I spoke to her, she was dating a Brit."

"Dating but nothing serious so maybe she'd want to show me the sights?"

I laughed, "Yeah, maybe she wants to show you the sights."

"Has she ever shown you the sights?" He asked.

"No Liam, she has never shown me the sights," I said with a smile.

"Good. Good to know. So, no bad blood."

"Nope, no bad blood," I assured.

Chapter 34
Ava

After moping for a few days, I forced myself to live life again. I had to. The holidays were upon us and I couldn't ruin it for the kids. Melanie and Nicholas had a wonderful holiday break and I returned post holidays, invigorated and ready to make changes in my life.

"What's this?" I asked, as Gina handed me a card.

"An invitation to my New Year's Eve gender reveal!"

"Oh, wow!"

"Yeah, at midnight we will have confetti canons with either pink or blue confetti. Team pink or team blue?" She giggled.

"That's awesome," I said, trying to sound excited.

"Yeah, right? Luke and I may not have any other kids and we figure we should do it all now."

"I love it."

"You're coming because of course, you are my cousin and my best friend. Besides, you need to get out of this rut. I'm tired of seeing you in this mood. Maybe you'll meet a new guy to start the new year."

"I don't want to meet a new guy! I don't want to meet any guys! I just want to go back to how it was in September before the Liam and Nicholas drama. I'm over it all! That's kind of what I wanted to talk to you about."

"Ok, ok, calm down. You don't have to meet anyone. Relax!"

"I'm putting in for a transfer," I blurted out.

"What?"

"I can't work for Nick anymore. Besides, he's in Paris now and who knows if he'll even return to Vilamor. I wanted to talk to you to see how you would feel if I requested a transfer as Luke's admin. If you or Luke aren't comfortable with that, I can put in for the IT department. Honestly, that might be the better option anyway as I will have less interaction with Nick and Liam in that department."

"I don't want to tell you what to do but I think this is a conversation you need to have with Nick directly. Not just for personal reasons but for business reasons. Structurally that may not work."

"Yeah, no, you are right. I'm just thinking out loud. I need a change in the new year. I'm just not sure what that change should be."

I picked up the invitation and read it, squinting as I re-read the venue location. "The party is at Nick's house?" I asked.

"Yes," she turned red. "But don't worry, he won't be there."

"Hmmm, ok, how did this happen?"

"He offered his house because we couldn't find any available venues in such short notice and it's so beautiful up there. Great layout too."

I nodded in agreement.

Chapter 35
Ava

New Year's Eve. I despised New Year's Eve. So much attention on this one day, so much stress into making it count and setting off on a great step forward into the new year. And the pressure! Could we discuss the pressure that is placed upon us to be 'happy' when the ball drops? We weren't all happy and we weren't all looking forward to what lay ahead.

As I entered Nick's house, it appeared that perhaps I was the only one not happy here tonight. It was awkward, perhaps even inappropriate to be walking through his house. You couldn't get much more personal than someone's home and he wasn't even present.

It was beyond generous of Nick to offer his house for Gina and Luke's party. It was beyond kind; it showed the level of trust and love he had for both Luke and Gina.

Most of his open floor plan had been emptied for the party. The furniture was moved to storage pods to make room for the guests, the DJ and the tables. Just enough remained to reveal the hobbies and joys of its owner.

As I walked about, I let my eyes take in whatever they could. He had an impressive floor to ceiling glass encased wine cellar. It housed both whites, reds and rose but I noticed his collection of reds far outweighed the other two. So, I concluded that he must be a red wine drinker. He also had a well-stocked bar. It didn't surprise me seeing the industry we worked in.

What did astonish me most was his love of art. He seemed to be an enthusiast of photography art, namely landscapes of Vilamor. The pieces were all images of Vilamor but as I walked about, it dawned on me that these were images of the places we had frequented during our summer together; the gold coast beach, the marina, the limestone rocks we used to escape to and the last one, the one that squeezed my gut was my grandmother's cliff or should I say what looked like the view from my grandmother's cliff. That view. There was no mistaking that viewpoint, that angle. It was all I could think about.

Luke came to stand at my side and admired the piece along with me. "Aren't these great?" He asked as he regarded the art.

"They really are." I lifted my hand, "this is the view from my grandmother's property. It's amazing! I didn't realize our little Vilamor had our very own renown photographer. I'd love to get a replica of this one for myself."

Luke turned to me with a dumbfounded look. "I'm sure if you ask, you can get your very own."

"Yeah, at what price? I'm not a Closter, I can't afford pieces like this."

"What do you mean?" He pointed at all four pieces. "These are Nick's. Nick took these shots. All of these are his. He took these pictures, had them processed and framed."

"Nick took these photos? All of these?" I asked in staggered disbelief.

Luke nodded. "Yes, he's always been into photography. I believe he would have pursued it if he wasn't a Closter and expected to head Closter Enterprises." Luke's words registered in my brain. Nick was a paradox. Every time I thought I knew him, I discovered something new. I looked at the art pieces in a new light.

"Did you see the piece above the fireplace? It is the largest. Must be his favorite." Luke nudged me with his elbow. I turned in the direction of his nudge. There above the beige-colored stone fireplace was an oversized framed print.

Unlike the other four prints, this one was black and white. It was an image of a woman in a white sundress standing on a dune, her dark hair blowing in the wind. I furrowed my brows as I took in the details of the picture, recognizing the young woman in the picture. That was me! How? He must have captured that shot during one of our afternoon outings.

I stared at the print, struggling to recall that day. It wasn't often I wore sundresses back at that age. As I took in the details of the photo, I remembered the dress. It was a bohemian, white eyelet embroidered dress that I had bought at the weekly town market.

It was a dress that Nick had spotted hanging on a vendor's tent and he insisted on buying it for me. He had said it was made for a Greek goddess and although I was barely Greek, he said I fit the bill and my association with him made me Greek enough.

Odd but at sixteen, I enjoyed that comparison and I remembered wearing the dress with pride. I also remembered how over the moon I was when he repeatedly complimented me while I wore it.

Vilamor, August 2000

The wind picked up off the ocean waves and blew across the beach, up onto the dunes where Nick and I stood. Sand assaulted my bare legs as the wind shuffled about my sundress.

The sky, although sunny and clear where we stood on the dunes, was dark and ominous out on the horizon. A sea storm was brewing out there and it brought a pleasing, raging breeze. Storms like these could be dangerous for those out at sea but from a distance, it was magnificent. I closed my eyes, taking in the ocean scent that the bittersweet breeze carried.

"It's beautiful!" I admitted, inhaling the beachy aroma and letting it penetrate every cell of my being.

"It is," Nick agreed, "but let's stay close to our ride in case we have to make a run for it," he suggested and I agreed.

"I'll go grab our sandwiches," he said, jogging back to the Vespa as I kept watch of the ocean.

The waves were becoming angry as they pounded into the cliffs with more vigor. Seagulls hovered over the beach as the beach goers started gathering their belongings to leave.

I looked back toward Nick. He was taking a rather long time to return with our sandwiches. What was he doing? When I turned, I was met with Nick standing by the Vespa, holding the camera up to his eye. He was forever fidgeting with that camera.

God only knew what he was photographing all the time. He brought it down from his face when he noticed me looking and hung it back on the handlebar of his Vespa. He winked, grabbing the paninis and jogging back toward me.

We looked at each other as we took seats on the warm sand. I fixed my white sundress as I crossed my legs pretzel style. "More photos?" I finally asked, not able to hide my curiosity.

He scrunched his nose at my question but didn't answer. I started giggling at his humorous look. He smiled and I could see a faint blush creep upon his cheeks. Was he embarrassed?

"The view was just so stunning; I wanted to put it on pause."

"Put it on pause?" I giggled.

"Don't laugh. I'm serious."

"Sorry, sorry. I get it. You want to have it forever to look back at."

"Exactly. I couldn't let it go unnoticed." I smiled with a nod. His hand came up toward my face and I instinctively flinched. "No worries, no harm. You just have a little mayo. May I?"

His hand was inches from my face. I nodded just before his warm hand gently laid on my cheek and he dragged his thumb down the corner of my lip. A tingling sensation ran through me. Then in an unexpected gesture, he took his thumb to his lips, kissing it as he took in the mayo.

"Delicious," he said. "You might have just turned me into a fan of mayo."

A glass shattered behind me, awakening me from my daydream.

"Be careful," warned Luke, moving me away from the shards of glass. "Someone just dropped their champagne glass. First casualty of the night," he joked.

And that was the day. I now recalled it, almost reliving it as I looked at the picture. He kept this picture all this time. My head was spinning. The all-consuming feeling of not being able to breathe led me outside to the cliff. I didn't know how I ended up there.

I didn't remember leaving Luke's presence. The fancy suits and evening wear were a blur as I started walking to escape the room that was slowly suffocating me as it shrunk around me.

I stepped outside, clutching my chest and gasping for air. I took in deep breaths of the cool ocean scented breeze. It resurrected me. The cliff, the sound of the wind and the heavenly smell that I could only attribute to Vilamor was a hug that I needed.

Something led me out there and as I walked past the pool, past the pool house and through the gated garden, I saw it. My grandparent's vineyard. It was so close. Nicholas' property abutted their vineyard. Everything was ok here. The view was just as it was when I was a kid. I wanted to go to the edge, reach out and touch the horizon.

I pulled off my heels, holding them by their gold straps and walked with purpose to the edge. It was dark out, close to midnight now but the moon was full, large, low and bright. It was bright enough to light my way to the edge.

When I reached that edge, I sighed, feeling at home. Being here and being alone, I finally allowed myself to cry. I allowed myself to release the weight, the pain, the burden, the frustration and overwhelming exhaustion of the past three years. For the first time, I truly let myself cry.

I didn't fight the tears or try to keep them in. I just accepted them and let the tears stream down my face. I was crying for myself, crying for my children, crying for all that they had missed and would miss. I was crying because I couldn't promise my daughter a happily ever after, because I, her mother, didn't have one myself.

I cried because she wouldn't have her father to walk her down the aisle. I cried because my son wouldn't have a man to play catch with or to talk about girls. I cried because of all the missed experiences they would have without their father.

All of this and more, ran through my head as I gazed at the bright ominous moon. I stood on that cliff and bared my feelings and thoughts as I had not yet been able to do with anyone.

"Ava."

I gasped. I was startled by the voice that came from behind me. My body jerked forward before a warm, familiar pair of hands clutched at my waist, pulling me back away from the edge of the cliff and toward him and his soothing embrace.

I allowed myself a few moments to stay and accept the embrace before turning to confirm my suspicion. Relief washed over me as I stared at the soft, loving eyes of Nicholas Closter.

"Nick," I breathed.

He ran his hand over my hair, caressing it and kissing my temple. "Ava, what are you doing here so close to the edge? This is dangerous. You shouldn't be this close, especially at night."

He was concerned for me, just as he was when we were kids. It felt good to be someone's concern. For too long, I was no one's concern. I laid my head upon his chest, relaxing into him and I wept.

"Hey now," he soothed, "What's wrong? Why is my girl crying?"

"Your girl?" I questioned.

"You have always been my girl, Ava. You've been my girl since that July day that you hung from that cliff."

I wept more. God, how I wished I had been his girl. God, how I wished I had chosen him. How I wish he had been the father of my children. But that ship had sailed.

"They told me you weren't in town, that you wouldn't be here," I said through my tears.

"I just got in."

"Why did you come back?" I asked.

"I missed home."

"Home?" I questioned. "Vilamor?"

"Well, yes but only because you are here. Anywhere you go is home. You are my home, Ava." A seagull gawked above us as it flew past. I detached from Nick to put distance between us. "I have been unsettled and homesick all these years not because I wasn't in Vilamor but because I wasn't with you."

"So, you came back."

"Yes, because I needed to see you. Ava, there is so much I want to say to you. So much I need to say to you. I need you to forgive me. Can we forgive each other and move forward?" He asked.

"What is there for me to forgive? You've done nothing wrong."

"I did. I left. I left and I know how that looked and I know how it must have made you feel."

I started crying again. I didn't want to but I couldn't stop.

"Hey now," he pulled me closer, rubbing my back and kissing my hair. "I know that my leaving must have hit a sore spot in your already bruised heart."

"You only left because I hurt you," I said. "I can only imagine what you thought when I left with Liam but nothing happened with him. I left with him because I knew what would happen if I left with you."

"I know, I know. You don't have to explain. We don't have to explain and I don't want to go back. I want today to be the first day of the rest of our lives. Nothing before matters. Whatever happened before today was just to get us to today. Can you do that for me? Can you move on and forgive? Can you take the leap with me and try this? Can you try us?"

"I can't, Nick. I can't be with you."

"Ava? Ava, I am begging you, please listen. Please, I've had the darkest days. I need you to just give me the grace to listen."

I shook my head, not wanting to listen, unable to give myself further heartbreak.

"You and I, we aren't that different," he continued. "We both have walls up because of past heartbreak, disappointment and abandonment. But I'm tired of being alone, Ava. I'm tired of running from love. Aren't you?"

"I don't think I have it in me to love again, Nick. I'm just not capable of it."

"Don't say that. We've been given another start, Ava. Don't you see? The universe, God, whatever you believe in or want to call it, has brought us together again. We literally collided, Ava. We aren't done."

"This is insane, Nick. You have a future, a wonderful future ahead of you."

"Ava, I want my future to be with you. My future will be colorless just as it has been these past 22 years unless you are with me. I want this life to be a 'you and me' thing."

"And if we try and it doesn't work out?" I asked.

"At least we tried."

I paced, rubbing my arms to both warm myself and to deflect from the pain in my heart.

"Don't you ever question what could have been? Aren't you curious what life could be if we were together?" He asked.

"Of course," I admitted.

"Right! There you go. I spent my whole adult life fleeing from one woman to the next, never satisfied because I was comparing them all to you. Comparing the conversations, comparing the laughs, comparing the fleeing moments. None of them measured up. I have never had deeper conversations or more laughs than I have with you."

"I have a lot to lose if this doesn't work between us. I have two kids, Nick. I don't think I can physically, emotionally or mentally take another heartbreak. My kids can't have another man come in and then out of their lives."

"That won't be a problem because I'm not going anywhere, unless of course you want me to."

"You understand that the kids and I, we are a package deal."

"Yes, yes, I know and I am ready. I don't want to be alone anymore. What am I working for if only for myself? Ava, if you will have me, I promise to lovingly treat those kids as if they were my own. You will need to be patient and I am sure there is a learning curve but I will do it because you are worth it."

"They are worth it. Tell me now, give me a word one way or another. If you don't want me, I will never mention it again but if you do—" I brought my finger to his lips, cutting him off.

"Do you like the zoo, Nick?" He furrowed his brows, clearly confused by my change of subject. I continued, "Growing up, I used to love to go to the zoo. I didn't understand why but I was always drawn to the penguins. Always cute and always regal." I laughed, remembering my visits to the zoo with my mother and my father, back when life was simple, uncomplicated and happy.

"Then when I grew up, I learned that penguins mate for life. They are drawn to their mate in an organic bond and once they find their mate, they return to that mate for the rest of their lives. Regardless of the distance or time they spend apart, they will always return to that one special penguin. Isn't that something?" Nick nodded, agreeing with my question.

"That is how I imagined love to be," I said. "That it was a guaranteed, always and forever thing, regardless of distance or time. You asked me once if I believed love transcended time and space. I couldn't answer you that day. I was flabbergasted that you asked that question because yes, I do, just as the penguins do."

"I believe it does because I loved you then. I loved you from the first moment my eyes settled on your face all those years ago. I never forgot you. I thought about you every day all throughout the remainder of my youth, even through my marriage."

I hugged him. "Yes, Nicholas Closter, I do believe love transcends time and space. And as you once said, I want to put this moment on pause so we can forever remember the day we found home."

"You saw the photo?" He asked, making the connection. "You remembered?"

"It's rather large and kind of hard to miss!" I said, laughing.

"You recognized it?"

"Recognized that it was me? Yes. A great moment frozen forever. It made me recall that's the day you started to like mayo."

"Ha! Not all mayo. Only the kind that escapes the lips of a certain sweet brunette that I have a liking for."

I giggled. "You're a good photographer, Closter."

"Thanks."

I perched on my toes and held his face in my hands, bringing his lips down toward mine for what I hoped would be the first wholeheartedly immersed kiss of many lifelong kisses and embraces to come.

And that was the story of how in the afterglow of our youth, after years of running, mistaken turns of events and avoidance, we realized that even though we had grown up, gone different directions and had different responsibilities, we were the same as we were then and our bond continued to be the same as it was. After years of living in a lost, melancholic nostalgia, we both found home again.

Epilogue
Two Months Later
Nicholas

The afternoon breeze carried with it the aroma of suntan lotion, which teased at my senses. The white sheer curtains that hung from my 12-foot ceilings danced in the gentle wind, letting the sunlight peek through as the rays hit the dark gray wood floors.

I moved the sheers aside and stepped onto my terrace, then descended down the three steps onto the pool level. I looked around, proud and fulfilled. This was what I worked for; this was why I chose this house. This home and this back yard had been empty and unused for far too long.

Now looking out at my yard, I watched as little Nicholas and Melanie splashed in the pool while Ava sunbathed at the ledge. It was a vision that I couldn't have imagined a few months ago. Their joy, their laughter tugged at my heart and I was happy I could give them this. I was in bliss that I had them to share it with.

That bliss transcended into work. I no longer yearned for the quick high I would seek from the constant flow of caffeine because when the stress got to be too much to handle, I learned I could talk to Ava, and she would bring me down from the ledge. The sudden onset of chest pains dissipated too. Oh, and those awful pieces of "art" in the conference room, that I prefer to call kids' doodles, have been replaced with my very own black and white landscape photos that Ava framed. Guess you can say my new life in Vilamor turned out to be better than I could have ever imagined.

"Hey, Nick, should we get the grill going?" Yelled Liam from across the pool. Yep, my brother was here too. He came home for the week for the Closter Enterprises anniversary gala and brought along Collette, his new assistant.

Sure, he was mixing business with pleasure but I couldn't really reprimand him as I myself was doing the same.

"Yeah, sure. Do we want to grill some steaks and shrimp or get takeout?" I asked.

"Let's grill. I'll grill. I can't grill in my apartment in Paris."

I walked closer to the ledge, hovering over Ava, framing her in a shadow. "Are you and the kids good with steak?" I asked her with a smile that I couldn't hide when she was near.

She stood. "It's perfect. Yes, the kids will eat steak and little Nicholas will eat the shrimp like they are M&Ms." She smiled, sliding her hand between the buttons of my white linen shirt, bringing me in for a hug. In her arms, I felt complete. Every time, no matter where we were or what I had going on in my life, I could hug her and know all would be fine. It was a feeling I had been deprived of for far too long.

"Ok, let's fire up the grill," I said, kissing her forehead.

"Will do with pleasure!" Clapped Liam as he lifted the grill cover. "I don't understand, how long does it take to have a baby?" Asked Liam.

Oh, that's right, Luke and Gina were supposed to be here today too but the baby had other plans for them.

"It's their first. Labor with the first always takes longer," said Ava.

"True, so very true," added Collette. "My sister was in labor for 32 hours!"

"You have nieces and nephews?" asked Ava.

"Just one, a niece, Isabelle. She's going to be one next month."

"Oh, well, Liam loves kids!" exclaimed Ava.

"Pushing! You're pushing, Ava." Liam pointed a finger at her.

"Just resting Collette's worries that if she wants kids, you wouldn't be opposed."

"Oh, unlike me!" I teased.

"You said it, not me," she laughed.

My phone vibrated in my pocket and I pulled it out as fast as I could. "It's Luke!" I exclaimed as I hit the green talk button.

"Hey, you're on speaker. How's it going?"

"She's here!" He said, overly ecstatic and in tears. "She's here and she is perfect!"

"Congratulations!" exclaimed Ava.

"That's awesome, man!" said Liam.

"Congratulations, cousin!" My heart squeezed.

"She's perfect and she's all Greek! She's beautiful. And Ava, Ava, are you there?"

"She's here, she's right next to me," I answered.

"Ava, we named her Francesca. We wanted to name her after your mom but we didn't need another Ava, so we went with Francesca."

"Oh, Luke, that's so sweet. That's beautiful. Thank you."

"So, we have another Frankie!" I said, looking into Ava's teary eyes.

"Yes, we have another Frankie. Hopefully, she'll grow up to be just like her godmother."

"Aww Luke, you're so sweet. Thank you. Please send my best to Gina. Let her know I love her and am over the moon for you both. I'll be by tomorrow to see how she's doing and to meet my goddaughter."

I hung up the phone, placed it back in my pocket and cradled Ava in my arms. "Are you happy, God Mommy?"

She laughed. "I am. I am very happy. I couldn't be happier and the kids are so happy. I love you, Nicholas Closter. Thank you for today. Thank you for yesterday and thank you for tomorrow," she said.

"I love you and I'll do anything to make you and the kids happy." Her smile was huge and it made me feel so fulfilled.

I never thought I could be this content but as my aunt Debra said, "Everyone eventually has their happily ever after."

~The End~